"You don't understand the danger," I said. "A bully, a mean teacher—"

She sighed. "I'll pay you double."

That caught my attention. "Double?" I said it like I couldn't believe she'd offered.

She raked her hands through her hair. "I'm desperate! Okay, fine, triple!"

Triple! Three bucks a day? The skateboard would be mine by the end of the month. The bell rang.

She looked at me, anxious. "Do we have a deal?"

I should have said no. She was crazy and the case was beyond dangerous, but I couldn't ignore the money. "Okay, fine. Deal."

Of course, had I known that by the end of the day, I would end up dangling over a swirling toilet, I might have charged her extra.

~ The Case of the Clingy Client

**Also by Natasha Deen**

*Sleight of Hand*
*Burned*
*At Dock's End*
*Guardian*
*True Grime 2: Angel Maker*
*True Grime*

# The Not So Secret Case Files of Billy Vale, P.I.

## by

## Natasha Deen

Alyssa.A

**The Not So Secret Case Files of Billy Vale, P.I.**

Cover Art by *Nicola Martinez*

Publishing History
First Edition, 2015
Print ISBN 978-0-9867419-9-9
Digital ISBN 978-0-9948763-0-0

Published in the Canada

*With much thanks to Johanna Melaragno,
Alana Eaton, and Nicola Martinez*

# Table of Contents

### The Case of the Clingy Client

In a school as big as Sir John A. MacDonald Elementary and Junior High School, things can get lost. When they do, I'm the guy who finds 'em. I'm not talking about the usual stuff like mittens or sweaters. I'm talking strange stuff, personal things. The kind of goodies that can get a kid grounded or land them in social skills. I'm good at my job and I know how to keep secrets.

The morning started off like any other. I swallowed my oatmeal and orange juice. Then I put on my uniform: jeans, T-shirt, a trench coat, and sneakers. I tossed the fedora—that's a cool hat detectives wear—on my afro, and I was good to go. Usually, I biked to school, but I'd popped my front tire during my last case. So, my mom drove me.

I made her drop me off a block from school. I love my mom, but she's got this thing about kissing me goodbye and yelling, "I love you, Billy!" through the open car window. It's embarrassing. A PI—that's short for Private Investigator—can't have their mom screaming about love.

It's unmanly.

I tossed my book bag over my shoulder and jogged the last block. Mom was in a real mood, today. She'd done that gross thing where she licks her finger and tries to fix my hair. Yuck. It made me late and I didn't want to get a note from the teacher.

I'm a good student. It's part of the job. The best kind of PI keeps what they call a "low profile." It means we stay out of trouble. Or try to. My job's dangerous. Sometimes things don't want to be found. And sometimes, the people who have those things don't want to give them up. Having teachers on my side makes life easier when cases turn hard.

"Hey, Billy."

I turned and groaned.

Slimy Sal, a short, skinny kid with long, thin, brown hair. He was the seller of black market merchandise. Black market: that's the stuff kids aren't allowed to bring to school. He had a rain coat that was stuffed with candy, pre-written essays, and toys. Sal sold his merchandise at expensive rates. A chocolate bar could run a kid three or four dollars, but they paid the price. If they didn't have the cash, they took out a loan—borrowed money from him. It was a good racket Sal had cooked up. A bunch of kids were in hock to him—that meant they owed him big bucks.

"Whaddya want?" I asked.

He looked around, then flipped open his jacket. Rows upon tidy rows of pockets lined the inside. They bulged with product. "Candy sand—pure stuff. Lemon, peach, or lime. Promise, I didn't dilute it with regular sugar." He closed his jacket. "Seventy-five cents for a gram."

"What!" I could buy a whole bag for a dollar at the gas station.

"Okay, okay, since we're friends, sixty cents."

I rolled my eyes and left.

"What about some gum?" He called after me. "I've got a fresh batch of Blusey Bubble Gum. Just came in this morning and it's got new packaging. Look! The wrapper's blue and pink, now!"

"Some other time," I muttered. I got to the grade five-six classroom just as the bell rang. After putting my coat on the rack, I went to my desk. Mrs. Robertson was my teacher. She had some weird ideas about doing stretches in the middle of language arts class. Plus, she liked to sing oldies music on rainy days, but as teachers went, she was okay.

Not like Mrs. Smith. She was a beast. Her rules. Her way. The thought of her made me shudder. She wore scratchy wool clothes and smelled of garlic and coffee. Plus, she liked to lean real close to kids when she was talking to them. I think it was just so she could blow her bad breath on us.

I sat down and listened to the principal's announcements. Then, it was silent reading, math, and social studies. I raised my hand to answer a few questions, and made sure I got a couple wrong. I'm way smarter than I pretend to be, but that's the life of a PI: pretending.

We have to blend in with everyone because that's the way we find out secrets and get information. It's what made me the best PI at the school. Of course, I was the only PI in the school, but that was beside the point.

When recess came, I grabbed my coat and ran for my office. Okay, so it was a red plastic tunnel that hung a few feet off the playground, in between the bridge and the monkey bars. It was quiet, though, and hardly anyone used it. I went inside, and took a spot in the middle. It wasn't good business to make my clients have to crawl too far to find me. Then I pulled out my notebook, pencil, and waited.

And waited.

Business had been slow. It was October, and I've found it always takes a few months for kids to need my help. I looked out one of the holes, and saw a bunch of guys I knew playing soccer. I wanted to join them, but I couldn't. A detective's always on duty.

A shadow fell across the tube.

I straightened. A client!

But then a girl climbed inside. I'd never seen her before, which meant she must have been new to school. She had brown curly hair, glasses, and freckles.

I resisted the urge to crawl away.

Girls never make good clients. Usually, when they lose something, it's a dumb item, like a necklace. If you listen to them talk, though, you'd think they lost a top of the line skateboard. To make it worse, it's usually not lost. By the time I start looking, they've realized they lent it to a friend. Then I'm out of luck and business.

I charge a buck a day. Not only is the girl finding her stuff no good for my reputation as a great PI, it's just no good, money-wise. Still, business had been bad and I couldn't ignore a client, even if it was a girl.

"Are you Billy Vale?" she asked.

"Yeah," I said, wishing I wasn't.

She crawled closer and I remembered my other reason for not liking girls. They smell funny—like berries or chocolate—and they're always worried about their hair. "My name is Allison Ranger and I need your help."

I wanted to tell her to scram. Too bad for me, I'd seen a great skateboard in the shop. If I was going to buy it, I had to take her business. "What can I do?"

In the distance, I heard the cheers and jeers of the soccer players. Sunlight beat down on the tunnel and reminded me that winter was coming. Soon, I couldn't play soccer, tag, or cement hockey. What was I, crazy? I made up my mind that no matter what she said, I wasn't going to take the case. The skateboard could wait.

"I'm in trouble," she said, "and word on the playground is that you're the guy to help."

She looked worried and part of me felt kind of bad about brushing her off. "Listen—"

"I don't know if you'll take the case, though—"

"Yeah, about that—"

"It could be dangerous."

Dang. She said the magic word. I love being a detective, but I especially love it when danger's involved. "Say that again?"

4

"Dangerous."

I nodded. This wasn't going to be a case of lost barrettes or lipstick. This was going to be good. "Give me the facts, ma'am—" That was PI talk for "tell me what happened." I dug out my pencil and opened my notebook to an empty page.

"I've lost a note."

"What kind?" I was getting excited. Sometimes kids forged notes from their parents. If I didn't find it before the school did, she was looking at social skills or worse.

"A love note."

"A WHAT!" The pencil and paper flew out of my hand. The notebook landed beside Allison, and the pencil ended up on top of her head.

I scrambled to get the book. It doesn't do for a PI to show emotion, but *gross*, a love note?

She nodded, not paying attention to the pencil balanced on her hair. "I wrote a note to someone and it's gone missing."

I reached up and took the pencil. Then I flipped my book shut. "You're on your own," I growled. "I'm a PI, not a love doctor."

"Please." She moved closer and sure enough, she smelled like strawberries. "You don't understand."

She had that same pleading tone my mom sometimes used. It was hard to resist. I sighed. "Fine. Tell me." I held up my hand. "I'm not saying I'll take the case, but I'll listen." I didn't open my notebook, though. I didn't need anyone finding out I had taken on a *love* client. "Start from the beginning."

"I just moved from BC."

*Speed it up*, I thought. *Get to the part where I run out of here and leave you on your own.*

"The first couple of days of school, it was hard making friends…"

I looked out the hole and wondered why I hadn't gone to play soccer.

"…was the only one who was nice to me."

Shoot. I'd missed an important piece of the puzzle. That's never good. Even if I wasn't going to take the case, a PI should always keep his ears open. Dragging my attention from the window, I looked at her.

"He was really nice." She blushed hard.

"You took his niceness the wrong way—"

She looked up. "No! Nothing like that. But I did— I had a crush."

Oh, *gross.*

"And I wrote him a note."

Double gross. I squirmed in my jacket.

"So, what happened?"

Her eyes went wide. "Before I could give it to him, I saw what a bully he was. Then I didn't like him anymore."

Bully. *Bully?* "Bully?"

She nodded.

"Chaz Menendez?"

She nodded again.

Oh, great. That kid may have been in grade seven, but I was sure he was lying about his age. He was huge—like twelfth grader huge—and meaner than Mrs. Smith when she's missed a cup of coffee.

"When did the note go missing?"

"This morning. It was in my backpack," she said. "The zipper broke and—"

"Everything fell out?"

She nodded. "A bunch of kids were helping me tidy up, but when I looked in the bag, it was gone."

"Do you know any of them?"

Her face scrunched together. "A couple, but not all."

"Would you recognize any of the kids if you saw them?"

She shook her head.

I sighed. Girls. They were always trouble. "I can't help you," I said. "If you can't even remember who was

6

there—" That wasn't true. If it was anything but a love note, I'd have asked every kid in school. First, because I believe in doing a good job. Second, because it would have taken days and that was money in my piggy bank. But no way was I going to go to kids and ask them if they'd taken a love note addressed to Chaz!

"Oh." She blinked. "No, a teacher took the note."

"Really?" I frowned. "Why didn't you say so?"

"You didn't ask."

Yeesh. Girls.

"She said that this was an institute for learning, not a barnyard for silly crushes and time-wasting daydreams."

Dang. There was only one teacher who talked like that. "Mrs. Smith?"

Allison nodded. "I'm in her class and she said she's going to read the note to everyone at the end of the week!"

That's when I turned and crawled away. Just my luck, she followed.

"Listen," I told her as I got to my feet. "You got to find somebody else." The fall wind rushed past and made my ears tingle.

"There is nobody else! You're the only detective in the school."

Shoot. What I wouldn't have given for some competition. "You want me to find a—" It was hard to even say the word out loud. I swallowed hard and tried again. "—love note you wrote to the biggest bully in the school, and take on Mrs. Smith." Then a new thought occurred to me. "Plus, it's October. No way Chaz was nice for six weeks straight. Why were you holding on to the note for so long?"

She blushed again and my gut—PIs always trust their gut—said she was holding a secret.

"What is it?" I asked.

She looked toward the soccer field. "I really liked him."

7

"So? I really like ice-cream, but even I know it'll melt if you put it in the sun. Chaz is bad news, and anyone with a brain could see that."

Her eyes narrowed and her face went red, this time from anger. "I was giving him a chance! To realize he's really good and be nice to people."

I rolled my eyes. Great. A girl *and* a bleeding heart.

She sighed, like she knew I was right. "I knew Chaz and I couldn't be friends anymore, but I'd kept the note for sentimental reasons."

I wasn't sure what "sentimental" meant, but I knew what "mental" meant, and I was pretty sure that word described Allison.

"I'm desperate."

"You don't understand the danger," I said. "A bully, a mean teacher—"

She sighed. "I'll pay you double."

That caught my attention. "Double?" I said it like I couldn't believe she'd offered.

She raked her hands through her hair. "I'm desperate! Okay, fine, triple!"

Triple! Three bucks a day? The skateboard would be mine by the end of the month. The bell rang.

She looked at me, anxious. "Do we have a deal?"

I should have said no. She was crazy and the case was beyond dangerous, but I couldn't ignore the money. "Okay, fine. Deal."

Of course, had I known that by the end of the day, I would end up dangling over a swirling toilet, I might have charged her extra.

****

The rest of the morning went fast, and when the lunch bell rang, it was my time to move.

Mrs. Smith's classroom was on the other end of the school. I scurried past the kids in the hall and made my way to her door. Allison was just coming out. Her eyes widened when she saw me.

8

"Stay cool," I told her. I checked to see if anyone was looking. Everybody was busy getting their lunches. Mrs. Smith had her back to the door. Quickly, I grabbed a piece of paper from my pocket. I wadded it up and shoved it in the spot where the doorknob met the frame.

"What are you doing?" She asked.

"My job," I grunted. "Let's get out of here."

We followed the kids to the cafeteria. The smell of day-old burgers and stale fries hung in the air. It wasn't a pleasant odour, but I was starving. Working a case really makes a guy hungry.

"Where's your lunch?" asked Allison.

"I'm buying."

"Oh. Do you want to get in line?"

I felt in my pocket and realized I'd left my money in my desk. "Never mind," I said, pretending I wasn't hungry. "I'm on the job."

"You should eat," she said. "Lunch is the second most important meal of the day. There's a big line-up—you should—"

Geez, she really knew how to annoy a guy. "You aren't my mother," I snapped, "and I'm not hungry." Right on cue, my stomach growled. I spun around and left before she could say anything.

I went back to the class. The hallways were empty and the area in front of Mrs. Smith's room was deserted. Perfect. The door was still open, but all I had to do was wait. When she came out and closed the door, it wouldn't lock properly because of the paper. Then I could sneak in, get the note, get paid, and get some lunch.

A couple of minutes later, Mrs. Smith came out. Instead of locking the door, though, she glanced at the latch in the doorframe. My heart stopped. She bent down. She peered hard and a couple of seconds later, pulled my paper out.

Of all the rotten luck, she'd spotted my trap. There

went my quick solution to the case, and my lunch.

Mrs. Smith snapped upright and whirled around.

I dived behind a wall and waited. The door closed. Her heavy footsteps came my way. I ran to the garbage can. It stank of banana peels and paper. I scrunched behind it and held my breath. Mrs. Smith came closer. Closer. Then, thankfully, the sound of her steps grew distant.

I peered out from behind the can. She was moving toward the teacher's room. I sighed and crawled out of my hiding spot. Then I went to her door.

"What are you doing?"

I jumped in the air. "Allison!" I whirled around. "What are you doing, sneaking up like that? I'm a PI. Do you know what could have happened?" I took a ninja stance to show her I was always warrior-ready.

She just rolled her eyes. "You seemed like you needed help."

I snorted. Help? Not from anybody. "I'm fine."

She raised her eyebrows. "Fine. Now what?"

"Now, you go back to your lunch and leave me alone to work."

"Nuh-uh." She folded her arms. "I'm paying three bucks a day, and if I want, I'll watch."

"No one watches me work," I huffed. "Leave or I'm dropping your case."

She stared at me. "I knew it! You don't know what to do. You work or I'm telling everyone you're the worst PI, ever."

She got me in the worst spot: my pride.

"Fine," I grumbled. "Watch. See if I care." I stared at the locked door. I was completely out of ideas.

"Well?"

"Shh! I'm thinking."

"You really don't have a clue what to do, do you?"

"Stop talking," I said through clenched teeth. "You're not helping."

10

She sighed. "Here." She handed me two paperclips.

I frowned. "What's this for?"

She looked at me. "What kind of detective are you?"

"The best in the school," I said hotly.

"The *only* one in the school," she shot back. "Look." She unwound the clips.

"Am I supposed to be impressed by that?"

She sighed. "It's for picking the lock." She glanced around, bent down. After she pushed the clips into the key hole, she poked around for a bit. We heard a *click* and her face lit up. "Ha!"

I tried not to look impressed, but that was a seriously cool trick.

She opened the door and went to step inside.

I pulled her back. "Don't be crazy!"

She wrenched away. "It's easy. We walk in, get the note, and get out."

I shook my head. New kids. I gave her the line my mom always used on me. "Don't be naïve."

She looked confused. "What does that mean?"

I wasn't sure, either. Every time I asked my mom, she told me to look it up in the dictionary. "Never mind that, now. You can't just walk in there."

"Uh, yeah, I can. It's my room."

I waved my hand around. "Look close. What do you see?"

She looked exasperated. "A room."

"A clean room." The desks were in precise lines, the walls gleamed. I think dust was too scared of Mrs. Smith to come into the class.

"So?"

"So, Mrs. Smith isn't just tidy. She uses all the furniture and neatness as a trap, to make sure kids don't sneak in the room and try to take stuff. It may look 'clean' to you and me, but to her, it's a security system." I pointed at the floor. "See that? How shiny it

11

is? When she comes back after lunch, she'll check. If there's extra sneaker prints, she'll know somebody's been in here."

Allison's shoulders slumped. "So, what do we do?"

"First, there's no 'we.' *I'm* going to take off my shoes and sneak in."

She nodded. "Okay, go ahead."

"Don't rush me! This isn't easy. If I go too fast, I'll smear the shoe prints that are already on the floor. If I go too slowly, then I'll leave heat marks. I've got to prepare myself."

"Prepare faster," she said. "Lunch is going to be over soon."

I shot her a dirty look. My stomach didn't need the reminder of its lost meal—I swear I could smell the cafeteria's famous burrito. Plus, I didn't need the extra pressure. I took off my shoes and gave myself a minute.

Allison huffed an impatient breath and shifted from one foot to another.

I gave myself another minute. Then I moved. Steady but stealthy, I crossed the floor. As I did, I tried to figure out how to solve my second obstacle. Mrs. Smith's desk. She'd angled it so the drawer that held all the contraband—that was the stuff she'd taken from kids—was pushed against the wall. I'd have to pull out the desk, but I'd have to put it back, *exactly* the way I found it.

I moved to where it stood, all the time, glancing one way then another. I thought, maybe, she'd lined her desk up with the kid's desk in front of her. I was out of luck. Her desk was to the left of it. How was I going to figure out how to put her desk back in the exact, same spot? Then I had an idea.

When I reached her desk, I took off my socks. I put one on the floor, next to the left leg. Now, I had a spot holder. Balancing on one foot, I pulled the desk out, grimacing as it screeched across the floor. I really hoped it wouldn't leave a mark. Gingerly, I tried the bottom drawer. Locked. I used Allison's paperclip trick and got it open. I wasn't as good as she was, though, and it took me longer.

"Hurry!" She hissed from the doorway. "Someone's coming."

Man, what was it with her and always adding pressure? I opened the drawer and rifled through. There were some cell phones, dolls, pencils, and music players. I couldn't find the note. Mrs. Smith would never throw it away and that meant one thing: someone had already broken in and stolen it. I was feeling pretty lousy, but then a candy wrapper caught my eye. An *empty* wrapper. Score! Mrs. Smith would never keep trash in the desk.

I took the wrapper and stuffed it in my pocket. Now, I had a clue about who had taken the note. I fixed the desk back to its spot, pulled on my sock. Going as fast as I could without disturbing the marks on the floor, I goose-stepped for the door. Allison shut it behind me.

"Well?" she asked.

I shook my head. "Someone's already taken it."

The color drained from her face. "Why would someone do that?" she whispered.

I could only think of one thing: someone had taken it so they could blackmail her, but I didn't want to scare her. So, I just shrugged.

"But—"

"You!" The rough voice of Mrs. Smith came our way.

I looked up.

She came at us, slow and mean, her face tight. "What are you doing here? You're supposed to be outside for recess."

I held up my sneakers. "I was having trouble with my laces. Allison was helping."

13

Mrs. Smith gave me a hard look.

I hopped into my shoes. Then I stepped back. "We should be outside, though, you're right."

"Hold it," she said. "You stay right here." She riffled in her pocket and pulled out her keys. She leaned in real close and said, "Someone tried to mess with my door this morning."

I blinked at the smell of garlic and stale coffee.

"You know anything about it, Vale?"

I shook my head. "I honestly couldn't tell you anything."

She stared at me, like she was trying to burrow into my brain and find out if I was telling the truth.

I was. I really couldn't tell her anything—not unless I wanted social skills and to have my folks ground me.

She pushed her key into the lock and opened the door. Turning to me and Allison, she commanded, "Stay right here." She went inside and looked around the room. Mrs. Smith took her time, moving precisely and with purpose. She bent down—slow and painful—and checked the floors. The she closed an eye and stuck her arm out, like she was lining everything up inside her head. When she got to her desk, she inspected it, and took an extra-long time.

I stopped breathing. So did Allison.

Finally, Mrs. Smith turned to us. She stared at us for what felt like hours, then said, "Go outside. And don't let me catch you in the hallways, again."

I nodded and Allison gasped, "Yes, Mrs. Smith," then we beat it down the hallway.

At the computer room, I stopped to catch my breath.

"That was close," panted Allison.

Too close, not that I'd admit it. "All in a day's work."

"What next?"

I looked at the clock. "Bell's going to ring in a

couple of minutes. I'll have to go to Plan B."

"What's that?" she asked.

"Confidential," I told her. "That means it's private."

She rolled her eyes. "I know what it means. I'm not an idiot." She said it like maybe I was. "I'm the client. You can tell me."

"Don't be clingy." That was PI talk for 'give me some space.' "It's for your own protection."

"You don't have any idea, do you?"

"Yeah," I said hotly, "I do. I'm just trying to keep you safe!"

"Fine." She shook her head in disgust. Allison reached into her jacket and pulled out a beef and cheese burrito. She handed it to me. "Here, for you."

"What?"

"You didn't have lunch. I figured it was the least I could do, since you're helping me."

I took the burrito. "Thanks." Maybe she wasn't such a pain, after all.

\*\*\*\*

The afternoon went slow. I was anxious to get started on my next clue, but it seemed like the clocks were going backwards. Even gym, which I love, was torture. As soon as the afternoon recess bell rang, I was out of the classroom and heading to Sal. I found him by his usual spot. He liked the grove of trees that stood at the back of the school. It gave him protection from the teachers and allowed his clients privacy.

"Sal."

A chubby red-headed girl was with him. She turned, startled at the sound of my voice, then ran off.

Sal wasn't pleased. "Look at what you did! She was about to be a paying customer."

"That's exactly what I want to talk to you about. A customer."

His squinty eyes narrowed. "What about them?"

"I need a name."

A slimy smile spread across his face. "I don't give out names." He gave me a meaningful look. "Not for free."

"I'm not buying information!" Actually, I would have. I needed the identity of the kid, but I didn't have any money on me.

"Then you're out of luck, Mr. PI."

I folded my arms. "I don't think so."

"Yeah?" He sneered.

"Yeah. You give me the name or tomorrow, I'll be in the trees with you. Only I'll be selling candy and toys, too, but at lower prices."

His face went white. "You wouldn't!"

"Try me," I said in my best tough-guy voice. I hoped he wouldn't call my bluff—how was I going to compete with him?

Luckily, threatening his business was the thing to do, because he said, "Okay, okay. Who do you want?"

I held out the gum wrapper. "Who did you sell to?"

He gave me an annoyed look. "Blusey Bubble Gum? That's one of my most popular products. Do you know how many of those I sell in a week?"

"No, and I don't care." I held up the wrapper. "This is the new packaging. You said you got it in this morning. All I need to know is who did you sell to today?"

His face wrinkled. "A couple—maybe four kids."

"Names."

"Aw, man." He dug into his pocket and pulled out his notebook. That book was as precious to him as his mother. In it, he kept all his records about who owed him money, and what candy was selling best. Sal whipped out his pencil and wrote down the names.

"Thanks." I walked away.

"What do you have?"

My head jerked up. Allison. Man, that girl was harder to lose than a shadow. "A clue," I said, like she shouldn't ask any more questions.

Of course, she did. "What is it?"

I sighed. "A list of names. Potential suspects for who stole your note."

"Let's see." She reached for it, but I pulled away.

"This is my job," I said. "Let me do it."

She rubbed her arms like she was cold. "Okay, sorry. I guess I'm just worried."

I looked at the names. Right off, I knew I could cross two of them off the list. Ruby and Jesse were kindergarten kids. No way they'd sneak into Mrs. Smith's room. The third name, Joe Fontane, was a possibility. He was the football quarterback, and liked to play pranks. It was the fourth name, though, that sent a chill through me.

Hank Shipley. Chaz's henchman. Hank wasn't smart, but what he didn't have in brains, he made up for with meanness and muscles. He loved beating kids up and pulling pranks. If someone had snuck into Mrs. Smith's room, it was a good bet that it was him. My heart sank. I didn't have a choice but to face him. I only hoped I'd have a face left, after he was done with me.

Allison saw my expression. "What is it?"

"Hank. He's probably the one who took it."

Confusion clouded her face. "Hank? But why—" She snapped her fingers. "Hey! He was there, this morning, when my bag broke. He must have seen Chaz's name on the note."

I nodded. "And he told Chaz."

Color drained from her cheeks. "Does that mean he already has it?"

I shook my head. "No. Chaz is in social skills, so he doesn't get recess breaks. He won't get the note until the end of school."

Allison grabbed the lapels of my coat. "Billy! You have to get it back!"

I pried her fingers off me. "I will. Yeesh." I may have been acting cool, but the truth was, I was scared out of my mind. It was bad enough to take on one of those guys alone. Each of them was three times my size. But taking on the two of them at the same time? I'd be lucky to have any teeth left.

If the time before afternoon recess had dragged, then the time after it went by too fast. Before I knew it, the home bell had rung, and I had to face the two meanest kids in the school. I wanted to sit in my desk, take my time, but the minutes were ticking. If I didn't get to their meeting spot, soon, I'd lose my case, my fees, and my skateboard.

I shoved my homework into my book bag, slung it on my shoulder. Then I raced for the boys' bathroom—the one by custodian's office. That's where Hank and Chaz always met up. Sure enough, I saw them going inside. Hank turned, checked out the hallway. I ducked behind a wall, counted to five, then peered around the corner. They were gone.

I stowed my bag in the lost and found box, then prepared to go inside the bathroom. A hand fell on my shoulder. I yelped—a manly yelp—and spun around. "Allison!" I clutched my heart, too freaked out to adopt my ninja pose. "What are you doing?"

"I came to help."

"How? By giving me a heart attack?" I dropped my hand. "This is a dangerous and delicate operation. You can't be here!"

"But it's my case."

"No," I corrected her. "It's *my* case."

"But—"

"Just leave," I told her. "You're just going to mess things up." I straightened my jacket and went into the bathroom. After making sure I closed the door quietly, I snuck along the brick wall and listened.

"—thought you should see it." I heard Hank say.

"You sure it was for me?" Chaz asked.

"Look." I heard the rustle of paper. "Your name's on it."

Oh, oh. He was going to open the note and I was going to be out three dollars. The potential loss of a really cool skateboard can make a guy do crazy things. I jumped out from behind the wall and said, "Don't touch that! It's mine!"

Chaz looked horrified. "You wrote me a note?"

Now it was my turn to look horrified. "What! No! I'm working on behalf of a client. Give it back."

That took him a bit to process. Then a grin slid across his face—the kind he usually got right before his fist connected with a kid's gut. "No. It's addressed to me."

"If she wanted you to have it, she would have given it to you." I held my hand out. "Now, give it."

He looked at Hank, then at me. Smiling, he said, "Okay, I'll give it to you." He walked toward me. So did Hank.

My knees were quaking, but no way was I going to show any fear. Just as Chaz went to hand me the note, Hank grabbed me. The bullies laughed.

"You heard what he said—" Chaz turned to Hank. "Give it to him."

"Your hair looks like it needs washing, PI."

I struggled, flailing my arms and kicking, but those guys were too big. They picked me up by the feet and moved to a toilet. I jerked one way, then another. Hank fell against the stall door. He lost his grip on me and I got my leg free. I wriggled, hard. Chaz dropped me. Then I did the kind of dangerous stuff that made me the best PI in the school. I snatched the note from his hand and ran for the door.

Too bad for me, Chaz has long legs and longer arms. He grabbed me by the collar of my coat.

"Fine," He ground out. "We'll do it the hard way."

He dragged me back to the toilet. Hank picked one leg, Chaz took the other. Oh, man, I was going to get a swirly for sure. There was only one thing I could do. I popped the note in my mouth. My plan was to spit it into the toilet. The water would wreck the note. I wouldn't be able to get it back to Allison, but hopefully, she'd realize that destroying it was my only option.

"Ready, little man?" Chaz put his hand on the handle used to flush the toilet.

"Stop!"

Oh, man. That girl really *was* harder to lose than a shadow! But this time, I was glad for the distraction.

They jerked at the sound of Allison' voice. She came into view. "Put him down!"

"You can't be in here, you're a girl! Chaz sounded shocked.

"You can't be doing that," she responded. "You're human."

From my view, I saw him frown. I tried to tell her that he didn't get what she meant, but my mouth was full of paper. All that came out was "mummph, mumphn, munf."

"Put him down, Chaz, and I'll tell you what was in the note."

He watched her for a minute. "Fine."

Chaz and Hank stepped out of the stall and dropped me on the tiled floor.

Allison looked at Hank and me. "Privately. I'll tell him privately."

I went back to the toilet, spit out the note and flushed it. "Fine by me," I said. "This bathroom stinks."

I went outside. So did Hank. We waited...and waited.

"What do you think they're talking about?" he asked.

"Believe me, buddy, you don't want to know." I folded my arms and leaned against the wall. A couple of minutes later, they came out. Allison looked okay, but Chaz looked sick, like he'd lost something valuable.

I shook my head. Poor schmuck.

The bullies moved down the hallway and Allison

came to me.

"Sorry I couldn't save the note," I said.

She shrugged. "It's better this way."

"So...I mean, how are you—?"

"Okay," she said. "I told him we couldn't be friends or anything else because he was too mean to everybody, and even though I had liked him—"

"No, no." I waved my hands in the air. I didn't need to hear any of that. Really, *really* didn't need to hear it. "I meant, how are you going to pay me?"

"Oh." She blinked. Dropping her book bag from her shoulder, she reached into one of the front pockets and pulled out a five-dollar bill. She handed it to me.

"I'll have to bring you the change tomorrow," I said. "I don't have anything on me."

She looked at the money for a minute. "Keep it," she said. "You earned it."

"Oh." I stepped back, surprised. "Uh, thanks."

She nodded. "You, too. Thanks." Allison slung her bag over her shoulder and went out the exit. I followed and through the window in the door, watched her for a minute. The five dollars felt good in my hand. So did helping out a client. I looked at the bill, then back at her retreating figure.

Maybe girl clients weren't such a waste of time, after all.

## The Case of the Fidgety Footballer

That night, after a really hot shower to kill germs from my time with Chaz and his goons, I went with my dad to get my tire fixed. The next morning, I was ready to roll. On the way to school, I rode by Ricker's Sporting Goods. My skateboard was still in the window. Good. Another few cases and that board would be off the shelves and under my feet.

I got to school and locked my bike on the racks. Then, I headed into class. The morning went fast. When the bell rang, I booked it to the office. I crawled inside and came to a screeching halt. "You!"

Allison looked up from the book she was reading. "Hey."

I groaned. "What is it? Another love note?"

"No." She closed the book. "I'm here to help you with the next case."

"What!"

"We made a good team, yesterday. I was the brains and you were the brawn."

"WHAT!" Did she just call me stupid?

"Think about it."

She scooted closer and I peddled backwards.

"I was your lookout with Mrs. Smith, and I helped with the lock, and I definitely saved you from a swirly."

"That's great," I said, not thinking that at all, "but I don't need a partner."

"Yes, you do. According to Lucas St. Cloud—"

"Who?"

"Lucas St. Cloud," she repeated slower and louder. She held up the book in her hands. "He wrote *The Art of Being a Detective*."

"Pfft. It's garbage."

"Have you read it?"

"No," I said, "but I know that no one named St.

Cloud knows anything about being a detective."

Allison sighed like I was the dumbest kid in grade five. "He's worked for the FBI, the CIA, and the NSA."

"Well, he doesn't work for me, OK?" I crawled backwards out of the tunnel.

She crawled after me. "Billy, he says it's good to have a partner."

"I've never had a partner, and I don't need one, no matter what fluffy McCloud says."

"St. Cloud."

I jumped down the wooden steps to the gravel floor. "Go away."

"You need the extra help. I've been thinking of advertising—we could expand the business, go beyond this school."

"I have all the work I could handle." I gave her a pointed look. "Right now, my hands are full with all kinds of problems."

"Come on." She was using the pleading tone. "It'll be great. Yesterday was so exciting. We could compare notes and solve cases. I had so much fun—"

I shook my head. "Dames. You're nothing but trouble."

Her face wrinkled in on itself. "Danes? Are you calling me a dog?"

"No." I scowled at her. "Dames. It's another word for girl." I'd learned that from a black-and-white movie my mom made me watch. It was boring—no car chases or explosions—but it had a detective who dressed like me. Plus, Mom had let me put extra butter on the popcorn and have a second mug of hot chocolate, so I didn't mind. "See? That's another reason we couldn't be partners. You're not as sophisticated as me." That was another word I'd learned from the movie. It meant "highly developed."

Allison glared at me. "Yeah? Well, Mr. Sophisticated, you have dried oatmeal on your chin."

I swiped at my face.

"You know what you are?"

"Patient?"

"A jerk! You're a big jerk, Billy!" Her voice cracked.

She spun away, but not before I noticed the tears.

"I thought we could help each other, but I was wrong! You're nothing but a doofus. An oatmeal-wearing doofus!" She stalked away from me.

I should have been happy to see her go, but in reality, I felt terrible. I don't like to make anyone cry. But couldn't she see? Detectives don't work in teams.

I turned and went back to my office. There were only a few moments left before the bell rang, and I figured I might still get lucky. Maybe a client would come by. Instead, all I saw was Allison standing by the doors. Kids ran past her. They dodged around her as they raced from one spot to the next. By the time the bell rang, I'd solved the case on why she'd wanted to be my partner. She wasn't looking for excitement.

She was looking for a friend.

****

Lunch rolled around, but I wasn't feeling hungry. My stomach hurt, but not because of a flu or anything. I felt bad for Allison. Then I felt mad because she'd made me feel bad. It wasn't fair. I had a job. Why did she have to horn in? Why couldn't she find her own friends or do something else, other than bug me? I stuffed my notebook and pencil in my coat and headed to the cafeteria. I knew I had to say something to her, but I didn't know what.

"Hey, Vale."

I turned, surprised. "Joe Fontane." My voice squeaked, but I couldn't help it. Joe was the quarterback for our football team, and the coolest kid in the school.

He checked the hallways, then came my way. Joe was a big kid. Not Chaz big, but big enough. "I need your help," he said. He flipped his blond hair to the

24

side and smiled at a couple of grade eight girls passing by.

They giggled and waved.

"What kind of help?" I tried to hide my excitement, but he'd never talked to me before. This was the coolest thing, *ever*. Joe Fontane needed my help.

"Professional."

I was in heaven. "Yeah?"

He nodded. "Is there some place private we can go?"

For a split-second, I hesitated. Honestly, I should have said, "Let's meet later," because I really needed to talk to Allison. Only, I still didn't know what to say. "Sure. Come to my office."

We turned away from the cafeteria, and I led Joe to the red tunnel.

"What's your problem?" I asked once we'd gotten comfortable. I had my notebook out and pencil in hand.

"You gotta find something for me." His voice sounded calm, but he plucked at his jeans.

"What kind of something?"

"A paper."

My heart stopped. "Not like a...love note or anything?"

"What?" He looked disgusted. "No!" His feet tapped a fast rhythm against the tunnel. "A paper I did for English."

"Okay." I wrote that down in my book. "Is it due and you lost it?"

"No." He shook his head. "I turned it in to Mrs. Larson last week."

I frowned. "And she didn't give it back?" That seemed pretty easy to solve, but I'd take the fee.

"No." He paused, and shifted like he couldn't find a comfortable spot. Joe braced his feet on one side of the tunnel, and reaching his hand out, grabbed one of the wooden posts. He pulled and made the tunnel swing

25

back and forth. "Everything I tell you is private, right?"

"Right."

"And if you tell anyone I can pound your face in?"

"Uh—" I didn't really like the idea of having my face made into burger. "I'm not going to tell."

I guess he must have been okay with that answer because he said, "What I'm going to tell you is totally private."

I nodded.

"No notes."

I erased his name from the paper and put the pencil down.

He took a deep breath. "We had to write a short story."

He stopped and I asked, "Was it a stupid story?"

"What? No! It was really good. It was about a dog who's a secret agent."

That sounded goofy to me, but he was a client, so I didn't say anything.

"Mrs. Larson thought it was really good."

I nodded and my stomach growled. I wished he would get to the point so I could get something to eat.

"She wanted me to enter it in a contest."

"Uh, okay…" What was his point? "So, someone took it and you want me to find it so you can enter the contest?"

"What are you, stupid?"

For that, I was going to charge him extra. "Calling me names won't make me take the case."

He sent the tunnel rocking, again. "Look, I'm sorry, okay? It's just stressful and stuff. Mrs. Larson was talking to me about it, but then, a bunch of kids came in the room. I shoved the story in my desk and left. The next day, the story's gone." He looked at me. "You see my problem?"

No, I didn't, but I told myself it was because I was hungry. The image of Allison, all alone, flashed in my mind. I had a feeling that if she had been here, she could have explained everything. My stomach started to hurt all over again. "Break it down for me," I told Joe.

"Look, I'm head of the football team, and I'm known as the Good-Time-Guy." He paused. "I think one of the kids may have taken it. Maybe they overheard me talking to Mrs. Larson and decided to embarrass me or something. If word gets out about how smart I really am…it's going to ruin my reputation."

"I don't get it," I said. "Lots of players end up in the CFL or NFL because they're smart—"

"It's different for me, okay? None of my friends are good at school. None of them even *like* school. I just want to fit in." He looked at me. "You do the same thing, don't you?"

"Uh—"

"Kids know you're good at finding stuff, but how many kids would come to you if they knew how smart you *really* were?"

"What makes you think I'm that good a student?"

He rolled his eyes. "You're running a detective agency. Duh."

I was feeling smart right up until he'd said "duh." I was definitely going to charge him extra.

"Look, just take the case, okay?"

I nodded. "It's a buck a day." I thought about him calling me stupid. "Actually, two, plus expenses."

He frowned. "What kind of expenses?"

"If I blow out a tire or something." Or decided to charge him for lunch.

"Fine." He dug into his pocket and pulled out two dollars. "Here. For today. If you need more, tell me."

"Okay." I put the money in my pocket. "Who were the kids that came into the classroom, when you were talking to Mrs. Larson?"

"Shelly, Raj, Hamish, and Simon."

I made a mental record of the names. "Okay."

He grabbed my shirt by the neck and yanked me close. "And remember. No one knows about the marks."

I nodded because I didn't have enough air to talk.

He let go and crawled out of the tunnel.

The bell rang.

I sighed. So much for an easy case. My stomach growled. So much for lunch. I headed back to class.

During math class, I wrote notes to myself. If I was going to find out who took Joe's paper, I had to ask some obvious questions. Stuff like, who had the most to gain by stealing his story? Did he have any ex-friends that held a grudge? To answer those questions, I had to step into grade eight territory and that was dangerous. Luckily, I had an older brother, so I knew how to act. Sort of. For the second time, I found myself wishing for Allison. She would have been good for back-up...she would have been good for a lot of things. Man, I hate it when she's right.

At recess, I went looking for her. I found her in her classroom, looking out the window. The smell of stale coffee lingered in the air.

"What are you doing?" I asked.

Allison jerked at the sound of my voice. She skittered away from the window, like I'd caught her doing something bad.

I looked around. "Where's Mrs. Smith?"

"Staff room. Said she wanted coffee."

Good, I didn't have to worry about her. "The bell rang a couple of minutes ago. Shouldn't you be outside?"

"I'm in social skills."

"Social skills?" I frowned. "You're not the type."

She shrugged. "I guess I am, now."

I looked out the window. A bunch of girls were playing tetherball. "Oh, I get it." If she was in social skills, then she didn't have to be all alone in the playground.

28

"Get what?" She shuffled back to her desk. "That you should wipe your mouth after meals?"

"Ha ha." I didn't say what I was thinking because it would embarrass her. So, instead, I said, "I get what you're saying about having a partner."

Her eyes lit up, but she shrugged like she didn't care. "You're a slow learner, but at least you get there." She took out the Fluffy Cloud book and rifled through it.

"You can't be my partner, though."

She pressed her lips together and ducked her head. "Yeah, I figured."

"What I mean is that you can't just pick up and be my partner. You have to prove yourself."

She slammed the book on the desk. "What do you think I did yesterday?"

"You made a good start, but you're still new. If you want to be a partner, you have to do more than read about detecting."

She rested her chin in her hand and gave me a dirty look. "Okay, Mr. Sophisticated, how am I supposed to become a PI if I can't work with you?"

"I didn't say you couldn't work with me. I said you couldn't be a partner."

She blinked.

"You can be my trainee."

"Your trainee?" She said it like I'd spoken Russian.

"Yeah. My unpaid apprentice."

"Oh, I get it." She rolled her eyes. "You're too cheap to pay me."

"I am not! A good PI thinks about the future, and that's what I'm doing."

She folded her arms. "Yeah, right."

"Fine. Don't train with me. Stay in social skills." I moved to the door.

"Okay, okay."

I turned.

The metal chair legs scraped against the floor as

she stood. "I'll do it."

"Good. You'll start—wait, when's your social skills over?"

Her face turned red. "Um, actually, I told Mrs. Smith I wasn't feeling good and wanted to stay inside."

I smiled. "I knew it. I knew you weren't the type."

She rolled her eyes again. "Yeah, you're a real genius. You should become a detective or something."

I sighed. Maybe this hadn't been such a good idea, but the decision had been made. Come tomorrow, I had a helper. I just hoped we wouldn't end up killing each other.

The next day, I found Allison waiting for me by the bike racks. She was wearing a hat that looked like mine, except it was pink. I wasn't sure how I felt about that.

"Mornin', Chief." She pulled out a notebook and pencil. "What are the orders for the day?"

Chief. I decided the hat was okay, after all. "We have to interview the client." I saw Joe playing goalie and I moved toward the soccer field. She followed. On the way over, I explained the case. "Privacy is what it's about," I said. "Not a word to anyone about this case or any other case, for that matter."

She snorted. "I know all about confidentiality. St. Cloud—"

I groaned. Not this guy, again.

"—says a PI's reputation is built on their ability to keep secrets."

I nodded. I'd agree to anything to get her to stop talking about Fluffy McCloud. Quickly, I told her about Joe's case. We came to a stop on the edge of the field. I made eye contact with the football player.

He frowned, waved another kid into goal, and jogged over.

"What's going on?" he asked, then glanced at Allison, and smiled. "Nice hat."

She giggled, that high, squeaky giggle girls do.

30

I sighed. This partnership was going to be a test.

"We need to get some more information," I told him.

"Like what?"

"Like who was around when the teacher was talking to you, who has the most to gain by stealing the goods, and who hates you enough to want to see you embarrassed?" Allison rattled the questions fast and out of the side of her mouth.

Joe looked at her like maybe he should have hired her instead of me.

"Yeah," I said, feeling lame, "questions like that."

"Oh." He ran his hand through his hair and I heard Allison sigh.

I shot her a look. Now was not the time for googly eyes.

She blushed and straightened.

"I get along with everyone—"

Allison gave him a goofy smile and I shot her another look.

"Anyone you may have had a run-in with?" I asked. "Even something that didn't seem like a big deal."

His eyebrows drew together and he puckered his mouth.

Allison started to melt.

I shoved my elbow in her ribs.

She grunted and gave me a dirty glance. "What about a girlfriend?" Allison asked.

I rolled my eyes. "Work the case," I hissed. "I don't need to go looking for another love note."

"I don't have a girlfriend," said Joe.

"What about an ex?"

Again his mouth puckered, and again Allison looked ready to plant a kiss on him.

"Shelly?" He cocked his head one way, then the other. "She was there when Mrs. Larson was talking to me, but I don't think she'd do anything."

His tone told me different. "You don't believe that."

His mouth twisted to the side. "It wasn't a nice break up, but—"

"Define 'not nice.'"

Finally, Allison was all about the case.

"The relationship didn't really work. She's nice and stuff, but she's everywhere I go, and it got annoying."

"I know how you feel," I muttered.

Allison shot me a dirty look.

"She's always trying to get back together, but if she took my essay, that wouldn't make me want to be her boyfriend again." He bounced his fist against his leg. "I mean..."

"What?"

"She still...hovers." He nodded to the left. A tall, blonde girl in a pink dress stood on the sidelines, her arms wrapped around her body, watching us. She turned and walked away.

"She drives me crazy," he said. "I just want her to leave me alone, but there she is, all the time. Just hovering."

"I'll talk to her at recess," Allison said quietly.

I nodded. It wasn't much of a lead, but it was better than nothing. The bell rang and we headed to class.

When recess came, I went straight to the soccer field. Allison was following one clue, it was up to me to find some others. I jogged onto the grass and heard a tiny voice behind me say, "Hey, what's up, Billy?"

I stopped and turned. Of all the rotten luck. "Hayden."

Hayden Small was a kid who lived up to his name. He was in grade one but was as tiny as my three-year-old sister. We'd met during one of the buddy-reading sessions—our class teamed up with his. He and I were partners. That was fine during class time or when I wasn't doing anything, but right now, I had a mystery to solve.

"Are you working on a new case?"

"Yeah." I turned back to the field. "And I don't have a lot of time, so…"

"That's okay. I can keep up."

I doubted it. He wasn't even half of my height.

"What are we working on?"

What was it with people and horning in on my business? "We aren't working on anything. I work alone."

His lower lip puffed out and his blue eyes narrowed. He folded his arms in front of him. "That's not true. I heard you hired a girl."

Man, news travels fast in this school. "I didn't hire her." I started for the field.

He stumbled to keep up. "So, why is she asking Joe's ex-girlfriend questions?"

I screeched to a halt. "How do you know about that?"

He looked at me like I was crazy. "I'm six. No one pays attention to little kids. I hear things."

Maybe he'd prove more useful than questioning the athletes. "What kind of things?"

He knew he had me. He sauntered over to the tetherball pole. "Stuff."

"Hayden," I warned.

"You let me work for you, and I'll tell you everything I know."

"Work for—!" I gripped my hat. "I barely have enough work for myself."

"And the girl."

"She doesn't count," I said. "I'm not paying her."

"You don't have to pay me, either." His tone was desperate. "C'mon. It'll up my street-cred. Look at me. I'm smaller than a four-year-old. No one listens to me. If I work for you, then I'll be important."

"That's stupid," I said. "You don't have to work

33

for me to be important."

"No." His voice was hard. "But I have to work for you if you want to get information."

The kid was squeezing me.

"I'll be your Guy Friday."

I frowned. I'd heard that term before. It meant an assistant or errand runner. I wanted to say no. I'd said yes to Allison and it was going to cause me problems. She was already making goo-goo eyes at our client, and quoting from a stupid book. Taking on a grade one kid seemed like Trouble, with a capital "T." But I couldn't say no. The kid was small, and I knew how that felt.

"Okay," I said, "but you do everything I tell you." I gave him a hard stare. "Everything."

He nodded eagerly. "You got it, boss."

Boss. Chief. Maybe this wouldn't be so bad, after all. "You said you had information."

"Rumour is, Joe's real smart and just pretends not to be."

My excitement dimmed. "I know that."

"Did you know he and his girlfriend broke up?"

"Yeah." Great. I'd roped myself into having an errand-runner. I'd live up to my side of the bargain, but I didn't think Hayden was going to live up to his.

"Did you know it was because of his friend, Samuel?"

My ears perked up, so did my spirits. "No, I didn't."

Hayden nodded eagerly. "Yeah, I guess they both liked her and Samuel made him choose. Their friendship or the girl."

"No kidding."

"No kidding."

Joe had been forced to break up with a girl, and the girl was still hanging around. Add into the mix a jealous best friend, and the suspect list was starting to grow.

\*\*\*\*

Lunch time came and I met up with Allison at the cafeteria. We went out into the hall, where we'd be alone.

"What did you find out?" I asked. The smell of hot dogs wafted into the hallway. My stomach rumbled.

"She says they're not really broken up."

"What do you mean?" I asked in a hurry-up-I'm-hungry-and-want-to-eat-tone.

"They pretended to break up, but they're still secretly together."

That took my attention from food. I thought about Joe. "He didn't seem like he was lying."

"Yeah, she's...I'm not sure I believe her. She said they leave each other secret notes and he sends her coded messages on the field. Like, when he makes a goal and puts his fist in the air, it's his way of saying 'hey.'"

"She's loonier than you."

Allison punched me in the shoulder. "I feel bad for her. It's not easy being rejected and I think she's made up some fantasy stories to deal with the pain. It's really sad." The line for food came out of the cafeteria and into the hallway. We moved aside.

"Do you think she might have taken Joe's paper because she thought it was a secret message?"

Allison shrugged. "Maybe, but I didn't want to push her. She's kind of fragile."

Man, I knew she didn't have the juice to be a PI. "You're supposed to push. That's your job. Do I need to talk to her?"

She gave me a look that could turn my milk sour. "I've got it handled. What you should do is talk to our client."

"Why?"

"If she said they were passing each other notes, then it figures he should have a bunch from her. If we read those, then we'll get a better idea of how crazy she was about him."

35

Shoot, she was right, but I did not want to spend my time reading love letters. "Maybe you should do that."

Her eyes lit up. "Yeah, I can do that."

"On second thoughts—I'll talk to Joe and get the letters. Then you can read them."

"Oh." Her shoulders dropped. "Okay."

This case was getting more complicated. I had a starry-eyed partner, an unnecessary Boy Friday, a crazy ex-girlfriend, love notes, and a jealous best friend. I figured there was no way things could get crazier.

Much to my stomach's displeasure, I ditched the cafeteria and headed to find Joe. I needed to get our conversation over as fast as possible. He was on the soccer field, eating a sandwich. His ex-girlfriend sat by one of the goalposts.

"Hey." I jogged over.

He looked up from his notebook and hurriedly stuffed it in his backpack. "What are you doing, sneaking up like that?"

"Are you kidding?" I crouched down. "You're in the middle of an open field."

"Everyone should be in the cafeteria, eating."

"Yeah, and everyone should recycle. What's your point?"

He scowled. "What do you want?"

"Evidence."

He frowned and looked at me.

"Word is, Shelly was writing you all kinds of love notes."

He ducked his head. "Yeah. So?"

"So, we need to rule her out as a possible suspect. I need to see those notes."

Joe watched her for a minute. "I doubt it was her."

"She thinks you're sending her coded messages in your football and soccer plays."

His face contorted like he'd eaten something bad. "I don't have the notes with me. I'll have to bring them tomorrow." He looked up at me. "It's not like I want to walk around with them."

I looked him in the eye. "Yeah, sure. Tomorrow." I stood and left. When I looked back, Joe's notebook was out again, and it looked like he was scribbling another story. Shelly was still by the goalposts.

I had meant to go back into school and get something to eat. But as I was walking in, I saw Joe's friend, Simon, walking out. "Hey." I stuck my arm out and stopped him.

He was a tall guy and thin without being skinny. Simon frowned at me. "What do you want, kid?"

"Information."

He snorted. "Go visit the library." He moved away, toward the blue metal doors.

"About Joe and Shelly," I called after him.

He stopped and turned around. "Who are you?"

"Billy Vale."

A faint wrinkle crossed his forehead. "The PI?"

"The best in the school."

His frown deepened. "Aren't you the only PI in the school?"

I ignored him. "Spill it. What do you know about Joe and Shelly?"

The wrinkle became a furrow. "Who are you working for?"

"That's confidential."

His eyebrows went up and he folded his arms. "I'm not giving out private information." He leaned in to me. "Maybe you're not a real PI—"

That got my blood hot.

"—maybe you're working for the paper and looking to dish some dirt on a sports hero."

And that got my blood bubbling like lava. "I would never dish dirt on a guy like Joe." I stepped close to Simon, so we were nose to chest. Craning my head back, I said, "I'm a real PI, and I need answers."

"I'm not telling you anything." His jaw jutted out.

"Fine." My voice was hard. "I guess I don't really need you anyhow. After all, I know everything—like how you made Joe break up with Shelly because you were jealous."

His hands dropped from his chest and curled into fists. "Jealous? Of Joe and Shelly?"

"You heard me. Word is, you wanted her for yourself—"

The veins on his forehead stood out, his face turned red. He came at me, hard, and backed me against the wall. "You take that back."

"What if I don't?" My stomach chose that time to growl.

He glanced down. "Then I feed you a knuckle sandwich."

"You don't scare me." It wasn't true. He terrified me. "You think I've got the wrong information? Then correct me."

"Joe's game was falling into the garbage pile. All he did was talk about that stupid girl." Simon pulled away and scowled. "He's always been crazy when it comes to girls, but she melted his brain. They even shared a notebook where they wrote their feelings." Simon looked ready to throw up. "I told him, if he wanted to see our team go to regionals, he had to get his head back in the game. He had to dump the girl—at least 'till off season." Simon stared at me. "But like her? Me? No way. She giggles all the time and—" His face contorted with distaste. "—she always smells like strawberries." He glanced at me. "I'm allergic."

"Yeah, I hear you."

He dug his finger into my chest. "Whoever you're working for, whatever you're investigating, it's not my problem or my fault."

I nodded and adjusted my T-shirt. "I get you."

"You better." He stomped out the door.

The bell rang. Shoot. So much for getting into the cafeteria for lunch. I looked around for Allison, hoping she would appear with food, but no such luck. With my stomach complaining about its empty state, I headed to class. I hung up my coat, went to my desk, and saw a hotdog sitting on it. I grinned. This partnership was looking up.

After school, I watched the football team practice, but it was dismal. Joe kept fumbling the ball, tossing it too hard or not hard enough, and playing like a two-year-old who was just learning the game.

"We have to find out who took his paper." Allison sat beside me. She pulled the collar of her coat up, and zipped her jacket shut.

I nodded. "If he doesn't get himself together, we're going to lose to the Rangers tomorrow, and McNally will never want Joe in their high school if he can't win them championships."

"Did you get the notes?"

"No, he's supposed to bring them tomorrow." I told her about Simon. "Did you find out anything?"

"Shelly gave me a bunch of notes she saved from Joe."

"Anything in them?" The coach blew his whistle and the team got into position.

Allison shook her head. "He writes a lot of poems about football...but I don't think he wrote her any of the newer notes."

Joe dropped a pass that even I could have caught. I shook my head. This was pitiful. We were going to get killed. "What makes you say that?"

"The paper's all crumpled. It's more like he was throwing away stories that didn't work, and she just took them out of the trash."

I grunted. More and more, it was looking like Shelly was the culprit.

"I know what you're thinking," said Allison, "but you're wrong. Shelly just isn't the type."

I snorted. "She's taking papers out of the trash and calling it love. Why wouldn't she take stuff out of his desk?"

"Women's intuition."

"What?"

"It means a girl just knows stuff. Shelly didn't do this."

I watched Joe get creamed by a pair of defensive-linemen. "Then who did?"

She shrugged. "I don't know, but there's more to this than an ex-girlfriend."

I sighed. We were running out of time. If we didn't find the culprit soon, it wouldn't just affect the game, but my reputation as a detective, as well.

The next morning, Hayden found me by the bike racks. I noticed he was dressed exactly like me. The only difference was that my clothing was wrinkled and stained. His stuff was perfectly pressed and so clean, I could still smell the dryer sheet scent.

"Got some information for you, boss."

I chained my bike up and asked, "What is it?"

"Possible suspects."

"Good. You have a list?"

"Raj Flavin and Hamish Tores. They're—"

"I know who they are—but why would his teammates want to screw up their star player and a chance at a trophy?"

"Jealousy."

Man, everything seemed to come back to that emotion.

"Both Raj and Hamish tried out for quarterback, but Joe beat them out. Word is, if Joe gets sidelined, the coach will split the position between the two of them. If they can play, then they'll have a chance at McNally, too."

The road to the CFL, and may even the NFL. Kids had double-crossed their friends for less. "I'll look into it, and...thanks."

He smiled and jumped off the rack. "No problem,

boss." He tipped his hat and strutted to the little kids' playground.

I headed to the field where I found Joe waiting. "Let's do this private-like," he said and led me to an alcove. "Here." He handed me two dollars and a thick packet.

I looked at the yellow envelope for a minute. A long minute. Then I said, "We think Shelly did it. Stole your paper."

His face went white, then red. "No way. She can be strange, but she—"

"She's been stealing your papers from the trash. Taking stuff from your desk isn't such a big stretch. I think I should report her to the teachers, too."

"Don't say anything to Mrs. Larson."

"Why not?" I did my best tough-guy imitation. "She could have ruined you. She should pay."

"At least let me come with you when you go see her." He stopped talking as Allison came over.

"Those the letters?"

"Yeah," I said.

"Hand 'em over," she said it tiredly, like she didn't agree to what we were thinking but she was going to follow the company line.

I watched Joe.

He watched me.

"Shelly did it," I said. "Case solved."

Joe's jaw clenched, and his Adam's apple worked up and down. "It wasn't her. You have to keep looking."

I shoved the letters at him. "This case is over," I said to Allison. "Go find us a new client."

"What?" They both cried it at the same time.

"You heard me. Over. As in done."

"You can't be done," said Joe. "You didn't solve my case."

"I don't work for liars," I said.

"What did you call me?" He stepped closer.

"You heard me just fine." I pointed to the packet. "I don't know a lot about love, but I know if you really break up with someone, if you really think they're nutty, you don't keep their letters. But look, you've got everything she gave you."

He stammered, trying to think of a reply.

"She wasn't lying about the secret messages. You purposely threw those papers away in the trash. You were still with her!"

"I didn't have a choice, okay!" He threw his hands into the air. "Simon was on me about her, and I just needed to shut him up. This was the easiest way."

Allison looked at him like he was the slimy stuff under a rock. "You were going to let her take the blame."

"No! I wasn't—I tried to tell you she didn't do it."

Allison shook her head. "Billy was going to accuse her, and you were going to let him. Some boyfriend you are." She shot him a disgusted look and walked away.

"My partner's got the right idea," I said and followed her, leaving Joe standing alone.

****

Shelly found us at morning recess, in our office.

"You have to take his case again," she said.

"No way."

"Please." She crawled into the tube and Allison made way for her. "You don't understand."

"He's a liar and he's got no honour," I said. "That's enough for me."

She looked at me. "Are you going to give him back his money?"

I shook my head. "No way. I did the work, I held up my end. He's just not worth keeping as a client."

"If you only take the cases of perfect people," she said, "you'll never have a business."

"How can you defend him?" asked Allison. "He was going to let you stand accused of the theft."

Shelly shook her head. "He wouldn't have."

42

"He seemed pretty ready to do it."

She shook her head again. "When push came to shove, you'd see, he'd have my back."

"How can you do that?" asked Allison in disgust. "He pretended you didn't even exist. He let people think you were crazy."

Shelly shrugged. "Sometimes you have to make hard choices for the people you love."

This conversation was getting grosser by the minute.

"You made all the hard choices," said Allison. "He didn't do anything but let you."

"Look," said Shelly, her voice impatient. "I didn't come here for a fight. Joe needs to get the paper back before the big game. He's got a shot at McNally and I don't want to see him fail." She pulled out a five-dollar bill. "I'll pay double."

I was going to say "no" because Allison looked ready to deck her, but my partner had a different idea.

"Fine," she snapped and ripped the bill out of Shelly's hand. "We'll do it, but not for him. For you." She pointed at the other girl. "This guy's a waste of time and if we have to solve the case to prove it, then we will."

"You're wrong," said Shelly. "He cares."

"About himself. He's ashamed to be with you. That's not a guy who cares about you."

Shelly opened her mouth, but Allison said, "Just shut up and get out."

The older girl watched her for a minute, then left.

"I don't understand what just happened there."

"Girl stuff," said Allison. "Don't worry about it."

I did worry, though, 'cause her reaction said that Shelly's situation was personal to Allison. When I hadn't been looking, somehow, Allison had made the jump from "annoying girl I know" to "possible friend."

"You sure you're okay?"

She pushed the money at me. "What's our next

43

move?"

I put the bill in my pocket. "There are two players on his team who would get his spot if the coach takes him off the team. Let's start with that."

She nodded. The bell rang. "See you at lunch."

When the noon bell rang, though, I was scouting for jocks, not food. I headed to the locker room. If Raj and Hamish were any kind of athletes, then they'd be practicing, not eating. Sure enough, I found them lacing up.

"Hey," I said, crinkling my nose against the stench of sweat and dirty socks. "We need to talk."

Raj barely glanced my way. "No autographs, pipsqueak."

I bristled. "I didn't come here for some stupid autograph. I came to ask questions."

"The press waits on the other side of the locker room door," said Hamish. "Wait your turn."

I sighed. "I'm not a journalist. I'm a PI."

Raj frowned. "A what?"

"Private investigator," said Hamish. He pulled on his jersey. "What do you want with us?"

"I'm searching for a missing item for a client. I need to know, where were you, two days ago—after the last bell rang."

"On the field, practicing. This is a big game, detective. If we win, we're that much closer to regionals and a national championship."

"Word is, you two were jockeying for the quarterback position."

Raj slammed the locker door shut. "What does that have to do with anything?"

"Just an observation."

Hamish squinted at me. "It's Joe," he said. "Mr. Charming must be the client."

Huh, maybe they weren't such dumb jocks, after all.

He cocked his head. "What did Joe lose?"

"Other than his mind," said Raj. They laughed and high-fived each other.

"I don't know how you guys can laugh," I said. "If your team loses this game, there's no chance for the championship."

Raj scowled. "Stupid Joe. He's losing his game and blaming us. Typical."

Hamish moved toward me, mean and slow. "What's he got you looking at us for, little man?"

"That's confidential," I said, backing up. "I just need to know where you were two days ago, and verify it."

Hamish's scowl deepened, driving deep lines into his face. "He's missing plays, screwing up calls, and it's our fault?"

"Hey, hey." I waved my hands in front of me. "Nothing like that. I'm just doing my job, guys."

"Every job has its risks, don't it?"

They grabbed me and hauled me above their heads. "Come on, now. You're really mad at Joe. Hurting me isn't going to do anything."

"It'll make me laugh," said Raj, "and with the way this team's going, I need all the laughs I can get."

They started for the bathroom stalls. Crud. Not again!

"Hey, Billy! You in here?" Allison's voice sounded from the doorway. "If so, get out here! The coach is on the football field and it sounds like he's changing the strings and plays. It might be a clue."

Raj and Hamish stopped. "He's changing plays?"

"We gotta get out there."

They dropped me. I fell fast and hit the cold, hard tile. I stumbled to my feet and weaved to the door. Allison and bright light was on the other side.

"Come on," I said. "We gotta see what's going on out there."

She checked her nails. "Nothing's going on. When

you didn't show at the cafeteria, I figured you were talking to the jocks. And knowing you, I knew you were in some kind of trouble."

I rotated my shoulder, trying to massage the ache away. "Yeah, well, thanks."

"Did they give up anything?"

"They're mad because Joe's screw ups on the field." I looked at the clock. "Less than three hours to go, and we're out of suspects."

Allison patted me on the shoulder. It was supposed to be sympathetic, but she hit a sore spot, and I hissed in pain.

"Sorry," she said. "Come on, why don't I buy you some trans-fat free fries? I'll even spring for the sweet potato kind."

Nothing makes a guy feel better than fries. "Okay," I said. "Give me a minute and I'll meet you there."

She went off and I leaned against the wall, catching my breath and thinking. Maybe we'd gone about this all wrong. I closed my eyes and thought about what Joe had told me: he'd been talking to Mrs. Larson about submitting his story to the contest. Then a bunch of kids came in. Joe shoved his story in the desk and took off.

My eyes snapped open. I realized who else had motive to take his paper. I went to the staff room and knocked on the door. Mrs. Smith answered it. The smell of spaghetti and coffee wafted past me and into the hall.

"Whaddya want, kid?"

"Mrs. Larson, please."

"Why?"

I gulped. "I have a question—" My voice squeaked. "—I have a question for her."

Mrs. Smith stood in the door and stared me down.

I held my breath and stared back.

Finally, she left.

I heaved a sigh of relief.

Mrs. Larson came to the door. She smiled at me, and I didn't care that she smelled like strawberries.

"Um," I stammered. "Joe said he wrote a story that you wanted to enter in a contest."

Her smile widened and I felt faint. I chalked it up to hunger.

"Yes, I did," she said. "Did you want to enter, too?"

"No, ma'am. I was just wondering if you have his story."

She nodded. "Yes, I took it out of his desk. I'm going to mail it in after school. Was there a problem?"

"I think he might want it back."

"Oh." Her face fell. "I hope not." She cocked her head. "You sure you don't want to enter?"

Now it was my turn to nod. "Positive, but thanks."

"You know, we're doing an Artist Night in a few months. We're going to set up the gymnasium with tables and those candles that look real, but aren't." She bent down and smiled.

I felt fainter and reminded myself to get some food as soon as possible.

"We'll have hot chocolate and popcorn. Would you like to get up and read something you wrote?"

"Uh—" I wanted to say "no" but the hunger must have overwhelmed me because I mumbled, "Maybe."

She grinned.

My legs got wobbly. "I should go." I headed for the field, remembered Allison, and went back to the cafeteria.

"Come on," I told her. "There's no time for food."

We booked it outside. Joe was warming up. Shelly was standing by the posts. Allison saw her and scowled.

"Some girls never learn," she said.

"You wrote love notes to Chaz," I reminded her.

"Maybe, but I realized what he a jerk he was in time."

I shrugged. "So, you're smarter than most girls."

Her eyes widened and she blinked like she couldn't believe I'd given her a compliment. Truth was, I couldn't believe I'd given her one, either. I jogged to where Joe was.

The sun was behind me.

He squinted against the light. "You got some information?"

I nodded. "Yeah. Mrs. Larson has it."

He frowned in confusion. "Why?"

"I guess she took your mumblings as 'yes, I want to enter the contest.'"

He took off his helmet. "Shoot."

"Yeah, she's going to mail your entry after school." I watched him. "There's time to take it back, if you want." I glanced over to where Shelly stood, all alone.

Allison followed my gaze. She walked over to the girl.

"But there's time too, for you to decide the right thing to do."

"Right thing? That's easy. Pull the story."

I shook my head. "All you do is lie. You lie about who you care about, you lie about your smarts. Maybe that'll get you into McNally, but that's all it'll do."

He scowled. "So do you."

I took a breath. "You're right, but I only do it with homework." I looked over at Shelly. "I don't do it with people. She deserves better than what you did to her."

"Shelly? Naw, she's a good girl. She understands."

I moved my gaze back to him. "It's not about understanding," I said. "It's about fair. And what you did to her wasn't fair at all." Taking a step back, I asked, "What are you going to do?"

We both looked over at Shelly. Allison was talking to her, and Shelly's head was bent low, listening.

"What do I owe you?"

"Nothing," I said. "Shelly paid for you."

I turned and walked away.

Allison came to me. "What's he going to do?"

I shrugged. "That's not our job. We found his paper, that's what we were paid for."

"We should do something, Billy—"

I shook my head. "It's not our place. This was about a paper. It's done. What happens between them is up them."

Allison looked back. Joe stood, staring at Shelly, who stared back. "I hope she dumps him."

Me too, but I didn't say anything. I shoved my hand in my pocket and felt the fiver. "Come on," I said to Allison. "I'll buy you some sweet potato fries." We moved to the school, and left Shelly and Joe on the field.

## The Case of the Pilfered Pocket

The past few weeks had been awesome. So awesome, I didn't even mind being wrong about Allison. It didn't hurt that Hayden was helping. For a grade one kid, he really got around. We were doing so well as a team, we were actually getting cases from other schools. Not much, one or two, but pretty soon we wouldn't be the best agency at Sir John A. MacDonald School, but the best in the whole city, too.

I got to school and headed for the playground, and the red tube that served as our office. Now that there were three of us, I'd have to figure out a better spot. It was getting crowded. Plus, Allison always had some weird, organic breakfast cereal that smelled weird. In a small space like the tunnel, the scent stuck to my clothing and followed me around all day.

I took my time heading up the steps. Frost covered the top of the red tube and left the wood playground frame slippery. From the corner of my eye, I saw a head poke out of one of the holes in the tunnel.

"Hurry up, Billy!" Allison shoved her skinny hand out and waved at me. "We need to assign the cases."

Cases. Plural. I raced up the wood steps and lost my footing. I slipped and slid down. My shin slammed against the step and my fingers got caught in the metal chain that held them together. I howled in pain.

Another head poked out of a second hole in the tube. Hayden. He peered at me, his little face scrunched together. Then he turned to Allison and said, "You shouldn't tell him to hurry. You know what a klutz he is."

"I am not!" To prove it, I tried to jump the last step. It almost worked, but I forgot about the frost. I fell on both knees. "Not a word!" I said through gritted teeth. "No one says anything."

Both of them retreated back into the tunnel. I climbed inside and sat down.

"Did you hurt yourself?" Allison asked.

"No," I muttered. "I'm okay."

She smiled. "Good because I don't want you limping or anything at the Artist Night—"

"I never agreed to go with you."

Her smile widened. "You will."

I groaned. Ever since she'd found out about Mrs. Larson's event, Allison had been bugging me to partner with her. She wanted to do a reading from Romeo and Juliet. I wanted to vomit every time she mentioned it. But it was getting harder to stall her—she could be pushy. Plus, Mrs. Larson had heard and whenever I saw her, she'd ask about the reading.

"Forget about that stuff." My breath came out in white puffs. "—what are the cases?" I glanced at Hayden and frowned. Usually, he's dressed better than most teachers. His mom presses his pants until the crease is so sharp, you could cut your finger on it. Hayden's hair is always done and he has this scrubbed look to him. He says it's because he used to model as a baby, and his mom's really fussy about how he looks. She thinks he might be "discovered" and become the next big kid model. Today, though, he looked...rumpled. His wavy hair was all angles and puffed out, his jacket wasn't zipped right, and his shoelaces were untied.

"You okay?" I asked.

He blinked. "Yeah—" He sounded irritated. "I'm fine."

I held my hands up, like, *okay, I won't ask any more questions*. "So, what are the cases?"

Allison flipped through her notebook. "The Lemon sisters—"

They were identical twins in grade five.

"—both have a crush on Simon Reilly."

51

"The football guy?" Hayden asked the question like someone was choking him.

My nose wrinkled.

"And they want us to find out which of them he likes best."

*Gag.*

"Eww!" Hayden scooted back as if he didn't want to be near the notebook. "Gross."

"You can have that case," I said.

Allison tapped the eraser part of her pencil against her chin. "Really? But you guys will miss out on hanging with the football team."

I shook my head. "I am *not* asking Simon if he likes the Lemon sisters. I'd rather *suck* lemons than ask that question!"

She nodded. "Your loss."

That's what she thought.

"The other case is for a kid named Finky."

My eyebrows drew together. "Finky?"

"Yeah." She squinted at the notebook. "Finky."

"I know everyone in the school," I said.

"Me too," piped in Hayden.

"—and I don't know anyone named Finky."

"Me either."

She squinted harder. "I'm sure it says Finky."

"No one in the school has that name." I grabbed the notebook from her and looked at the paper. "Holy smokes. That's the worst handwriting I've ever seen. Hayden could do better."

"And I don't even write," he said.

"Give me a break." She ripped the notebook out of my hands. "I was running to catch the bus, okay?"

I shrugged. Then I looked over her shoulder. "That might be an 'S' not an 'F.'"

"Sinky?" Hayden's nose wrinkled. "No one's named Sinky in the school, either."

I shifted, trying to find a comfortable spot in the cramped space. As I grabbed the edge of one of the windows in the tunnel, I saw a figure move under us.

"Did you see that?" I asked.

"Yeah, I did," Alison said, "but who would be at school this early?"

I stuck my head out of the entrance, but no one was there. Then I crawled to the other side and looked out. Still, no one.

Hayden looked out the window. "I don't see anybody."

We watched each other. The whole reason we met this early was so we'd be alone. No kids would be around to hear our conversations, and none of the teachers would be on the playground until ten minutes before first bell.

I poked my head out the tunnel. "No one could just disappear like that," I said.

Allison craned her head out of one of the windows and peered down. "No one's around here, either."

"Maybe it was a bird or something," said Hayden.

"Awful big bird," murmured Allison.

A creepy feeling ran over me.

We exchanged looks, then crawled toward the opening of the tunnel.

"We can keep talking about this inside," I said. "I'm not scared or anything—"

"Me neither," said Allison, "but my fingers are cold."

"Yeah," said Hayden. "Me too."

We got out and scrambled down the steps. Our feet crunched against the gravel. Allison scurried ahead. Hayden was beside her.

Truthfully, I was freaked, but I didn't want to let on, so I took my time. I walked slowly, even though my heart thumped in my chest.

"Hey—"

A raspy voice reached out to me and someone grabbed my shoulder.

I yelped, twisted, and turned around. "Holy

smokes! Sal!" I clutched my chest and caught my breath. "You're lucky I realized it was you." I took my ninja pose. "You could have been hurt."

A toothpick dangled from the side of his mouth. His beady, black eyes looked me up and down. "Yeah," he said, as he flicked the toothpick to the ground. "I can tell you're a real lethal weapon."

"Hey," said Allison, "that's littering."

His gaze jumped to her then back to me.

I flipped the collar of my trench coat up. "What do you want?"

"Your help."

Allison stomped toward us. "What kind of help?"

"Professional."

She folded her arms and glared down at him. "Pick up the toothpick and we'll talk."

"I'm not picking it up!"

"Then we're not helping you." She turned on her heel, spraying pebbles. "Come on, guys."

"Uh—" Hayden and I looked at each other. Not taking a case because of a toothpick seemed like a dumb reason, but Allison was a girl, and girls can be crazy when they're mad at you.

"I said, come on!" Her words snapped in the cold air.

My decision was made. "Sorry, Sal, but she brings lunch and clients. Can't mess with that."

"Aw, for all the—" He bent down and grabbed the toothpick. Holding it up, he yelled, "Are you happy now? See?"

She shrugged, like it was no big deal. "What do you want?"

"Discreet help."

Hayden's forehead wrinkled. "Dis-what?"

"It means he wants our help, but he doesn't want anyone to know we're helping him."

"Oh," said Hayden, looking at Sal. "Why didn't you just say so?"

The older kid sighed. "I did. Look—Vale, you gonna help me, or what?"

"Sure," I said. "I'll help. Come on, let's go stand outside the main doors. The tunnel's too small for us to fit in."

We trudged to the blue doors.

"It's freezing," said Allison, blowing on her fingers. "Let's go inside. The teachers won't kick us out until later."

It was a good idea, but that was the thing with her. She always had good ideas. We hurried to the entrance and scurried inside. Warm heat made my ears tingle and the toasty smell of the furnace wafted from the overhead vent.

"What's going on?" I asked Sal.

"Someone's stolen my book," he said, as he leaned against the cement wall.

"A library book?" asked Hayden.

"No," I said. "His record book."

Confusion blurred the kid's eyes.

"Sal sells black market stuff—candy, pop, homework answers—"

"I know that," Hayden scoffed. "Every kid does."

"Right, but he has to keep a record of who is buying from him, and what they're buying—"

Hayden's eyes cleared. "The record book."

Allison flipped open her notebook, licked the tip of her pencil, and said, "Give me the facts."

"I don't just keep buyer records in that book," said Sal. "I keep a list of my entire inventory."

He got three blank stares.

"It's like this—" He took Allison's book.

We crowded around him.

Using her pencil, he drew five circles. "Let's say each of these circles represents something I sell. One circle is candy, one is pop, one is forged notes so kids can get out of class. Now—" Inside each circle, he drew smaller circles. "—candy isn't just candy. It's

55

gummy bears, chocolate, chocolate with fruit. I have to keep track of everything so I know what's selling." He handed the book back to Allison. "A dealer is only as good as the supplies he has. If I run out of bubble gum, those kids'll go to someone else for their product. I won't just lose that sale, I might lose their business if they decide to stick with their new guy."

"Okay."

"No, it's not okay!"

He did a weird chicken-strut-walk to a set of shoe shelves, then back to us.

"It's a disaster! If I can't find the book, my whole business is messed up." His face pulled into tortured lines. "I'll never pay for college."

"College?" Both Allison and I asked the question, surprised.

"Of course. Why do you think I do all this? For my health? I need money, man. It's just me and Mom, and she can't afford to send me to university or anything. I'm going to be a big-deal businessman. This stuff—selling candy and pop—it isn't great, but it's experience. It gives me a chance to see how people buy stuff, the kinds of things that sell, and it's going to my college fund so I can get into a great school."

I blinked. Then I blinked again. I'd never thought of Sal as having ambition or dreams. From the astonished expression on Allison's face, she'd never thought of it, either.

"This weekend, I'm supposed to check my inventory," said Sal. "I do it every three months, but without the book, I won't know what's going on. How am I going to stock my candy if I don't know which ones are more popular?" He raised his hands, then dropped them to his sides. "And what am I going to do about all those fake notes? If the office starts getting too many 'Please let me kid out of school early for a dentist appointment,' they're going to get suspicious."

"It's going to be okay," said Allison. "We're on the

job." Her pen hovered over the paper. "Start at the beginning. When did you last have the book?"

"Friday," he said, "two days ago."

"You're sure?"

"Yeah," he said, irritated. "I'm sure. Ky, Christopher, and I were going to the Game-O-Rama."

"The one in West Edmonton Mall? By Mulligan's Treats?"

He nodded. "I checked my book, saw I needed to stock up on lollipops. Then, I stuck the book back in my pocket, patted it—"

His gaze went unfocused, as though he was looking into the past.

"—I always pat my coat, to make sure the book's in there." He shrugged. "I was at the Game-O-Rama for a couple of hours, then went home. I didn't check my coat until last night, when I was getting ready for school."

"We'll need to investigate the Game-O-Rama," said Allison. "See if anything was turned into their Lost and Found."

I nodded. "Okay, Sal, we'll take the case."

"Usual rates?"

I nodded again. "Yeah, a buck a day, plus expenses."

"Expense?"

"Yeah, if we have to take a bus or something."

"Oh," he said. "Okay." He dug into his coat pocket and pulled out a five-dollar bill. "Here," he said. "To make sure you work for me, and keep your mouths shut."

I took the bill.

"I want daily updates, Vale. I'll send Ky and Christopher to talk to you. Maybe they saw something."

I nodded.

"Good." He flipped the collar of his coat. "Gotta get out there. Kids will start to wonder if I'm not at my usual spot." He left, pushing the door open. A gust of cold wind set the leaves scattering inside.

"If we're supposed to keep everything quiet," asked Hayden, "how are we going to ask around?"

"Let's do some checking first," I said, "before we start asking kids about it."

"After school—"Allison slid her pencil into the spiral loops of her notebook, "—we'll meet here and head to Game-O-Rama."

"In the meantime," I said, "keep your ears open. Maybe someone saw something."

****

After school, I met Allison and Hayden at the doors that opened to the soccer field.

"Anything?" I asked.

They both shook their heads.

"I figure it's a simple matter of a lost notebook. If it's not at the lost and found, it was probably swept up with the trash," I said

Allison shuddered. "Tell me we're not going dumpster-diving."

"What's that?" asked Hayden.

"It means we climb into a dumpster and root through the garbage and look for his notebook."

His nose wrinkled. "Are we seriously going to do that? My mom'll freak." He froze for a moment, then the scrunched look on his face smoothed out. "I'll do it."

I frowned. It wasn't like Hayden to do stuff to make his mom mad. "You sure you're okay?"

"Yeah." The irritated tone was back. "Quit asking."

*Oookkkaaay.* "Allison, did you bring your bike?"

She nodded.

"Hayden?"

He nodded, too.

"Okay." I stepped outside and headed to the bike rake. "Let's go."

They got their bikes, helmets, and pretty soon, we

were hurtling down the sidewalk of one-seventy-eight street, and speeding toward West Edmonton Mall.

"We should figure out a plan," said Allison. "For once we get there."

I shrugged. "Go to the Lost and Found, and find the book."

"What if it's not there?" The wind made her curly hair stream back from her face and turned her cheeks red. "I'm not going into a dumpster."

Truthfully, I didn't want too, either. "Maybe we won't have too," I said. "At least, not right away. They have all kinds of cameras in the building. Maybe we can get a look at the footage."

Allison shot me one of her trademark "boy, are you dumb" looks. "You can't just go in and ask. My mom's a lawyer and she says you need something called a subpoena to get stuff like that."

"A sup-eena?"

She nodded. "It's a piece of paper the courts give to cops and it lets them take stuff out of people's homes and businesses."

Hayden glanced at her.

"Cops just can't go into a building and take stuff. People have a right to privacy. Police need permission." She looked at me. "And if the police need permission, what do you think the Game-O-Rama security is going to say when a bunch of kids ask to review footage from yesterday?"

Hmm, good point. "Okay, let me think on it."

It took ten minutes to get to Game-O-Rama, but the time hadn't done anything to help me come up with a plan. I still didn't know what I'd do if we didn't find the notebook. We pulled up to the glass and metal doors.

Game-O-Rama was a three-story monster of a building. It had an outside elevator that went from the roof to the ground. It had a glass floor, seatbelts, and no walls, and it dropped a kid to the ground in less than

three seconds. Everyone knew two things about this
ride: never eat *anything* before climbing on. Second, if
the ride was going, don't be near the drop point,
because if a kid threw up, it would splatter everywhere.

After we chained our bikes, we went inside the
glass-and-metal doors.

On the right were the usual games: Whack a Mole,
basketball, and bowling. On the left was the arcade, and
straight ahead was laser tag. Even though school had
just let out, the place was already packed with kids
spending their money, and collecting their tickets for
prizes.

Overhead bells went off, whistles sounded, and
lights pulsed. Dance music thumped from hidden
speakers and over all that, was the noise of screaming
kids. The smell of burgers, pizza, and fries covered the
room like an oily blanket. I went to the back because
that's where the Lost and Found was.

A bored teenager with a wispy beard, and a death
metal black shirt sat behind the counter.

"Hey," I said.

He popped his pink bubble gum and looked at me
from over the top of his science-fiction magazine.

"I think I lost my notebook here. Can I check the
lost and found?"

He shook his head. "No can do, *amigo*, but if you
describe the notebook, I can check for you."

"It's black," said Allison, "and it's about four
inches by six inches."

He disappeared into the back room. After a few
minutes, he came back. "Nothing's there."

"Are you sure?" Allison pressed her hands against
the scarred counter. "It's really important, and it has
numbers in it—"

The guy looked at her, his eyes narrowed into slits.
He turned his gaze to me, then back to her. "Whose
book is this, anyway? Yours or hers?"

"Mine." We both answered.

His wispy eyebrows went up.

"It's both of ours," said Allison. "It's for a group project and if we don't find it, then I'm going to fail. Please—"

She did that girl-thing, where they make their eyes all liquid and gooey.

"—I've never failed anything in my life. I'm an A-student."

His face softened with sympathy.

Man, she was good.

"I'll go and check again." He disappeared into the back.

Allison shot me a triumphant glance that made her lips turn up and her cheeks flush.

"Yeah, yeah," I said. "Don't brag."

The guy was gone for a long time, but when he finally came out, his hands were empty.

"I'm sorry," he said. "It's just not there."

"Are you sure?" I asked. "The room's big—can't I go back and check?"

He shook his head. "The room's not just for Lost and Found. It's for storage, too."

Allison's eyes turned liquid, again.

He watched her for a minute, his lips pressed together.

She tilted her head. "Please."

He sighed. "Look, I tell you what. I'll go get the box and bring it out here. You can search."

She gave him a look like he'd just saved her puppy from a runaway car and said, "Thanks. You're the best."

He blushed, mumbled, "Uh, yeah. Sure," and scurried into the back.

She gave me another triumphant smile.

I rolled my eyes. "Yeah, yeah."

"Geez. I did a great job. Didn't you see—"

"Yeah, I did," I snapped, "but you don't have to brag."

Her eyebrows wrinkled and she shot me a dirty look. "I wasn't—"

I snorted.

"I was just…"

I rolled my eyes.

"Fine," she said, her voice hard. "Never mind."

The Lost and Found guy returned with a cardboard box. Sweaters, caps, and backpacks flowed over the top.

"Here," he said. "Have at 'er."

Allison took the task. Deliberately, she removed every item, one at a time. She patted down the sweaters, checked inside the caps, and looked in the pockets of the backpacks. Then she did it again. After the third time, she placed the last item back in the box and said, "You're right. It's not here."

He shrugged. "I'm sorry."

We moved away. "Now what?"

"We'll have to figure out a way to check the security cameras," I said.

She nodded. Then she frowned. She looked left, right, then behind her. "Where's Hayden?"

"He's right—" I checked the room. "Great," I grumbled. "Some help. He gets into the arcade and forgets about the case."

Allison frowned. "That's not like him."

"Come on," I said. "He's probably at one of the games."

We left the Lost and Found room and the sounds of the arcade drowned the chance to talk. I pointed left, meaning I'd go that way. Then I pointed right, meaning Allison should take that direction and look for Hayden.

She nodded.

I went left.

So did she, and we collided.

I staggered back. "What are you doing?" I had to yell to be heard over the music, games, and kids.

"Going left."

62

She was using her "boy, are you dumb voice" again.

"That's what you said to do."

"No, I'll go left. You go right."

She rolled her eyes and moved away.

I looped the Game-O-Rama, but I couldn't find him. I saw Allison standing by the prize counter and went to her.

"Any luck?" I shouted the question.

She shook her head.

"I can't believe he bailed." My face wrinkled with disgust. "Some big help."

"He's not like that," Allison snapped. "I think something's happened."

"Like what?"

"Like I don't know." She had an edge in her voice sharp enough to cut paper. "But Hayden's a good kid who wants to be just like you." She shot me a dirty look. "Though, I can't understand why." She scanned the room and worry replaced scorn. "He wouldn't just take off." Allison pursed her lips. "I think we should check with security."

"That's not a bad idea," I said. "Maybe we can see if they'll let us look at the other footage."

Contempt contorted her face. "Don't you ever think of anyone besides yourself?" She shoved her finger into my chest.

"What are you talking about?" I resisted the urge to rub the spot she'd poked. It hurt—a lot—but I didn't want her to know that. "I'm thinking about my client."

"*Your* client." She shook her head. "Honestly." She strode toward the security office.

I raced to catch up. "What's your problem?"

"You," she snarled. "You're my problem."

Her words stung. "If you're having such a rough time of it, then you can always leave."

"Hayden's my friend," she said through clenched teeth. "I'm not going anywhere until I know he's okay."

She came to an abrupt stop in front of the grey doors of the security office. Raising her hand, she knocked.

After a couple of seconds, the door opened.

A uniformed guard, probably the age of my grandfather, answered. He had grizzled white, curly hair that rimmed his shiny, bald dome. The guard smiled and in a raspy voice asked, "Yes?"

"I can't find my friend—"

"Allison!"

The door swung open and we saw Hayden.

Allison's face went slack with relief. Then it turned red. "Why did you just take off like that? We didn't know where you were!"

He cocked his head. "I didn't take off. I told you guys I was going to talk to security."

"No way." I shook my head. "You didn't say anything."

"Yeah," he insisted. "I did. It was right after the guy left. You were just too busy arguing about if Allison was bragging to hear me."

Allison and I exchanged looks.

"Oh," she said. "I'm sorry I wasn't paying attention."

"It's okay." He beamed at the security guard. "Dennis's been helping me with my passion project."

Uhh...I glanced at Allison.

"You know—" Hayden leaned toward us, and put extra emphasis on the words. "My *passion* project."

"Oh, yeah, right." I forced a laugh and said to the guard, "He's just a smart kid. It's hard to keep up with all his projects." I turned back to Hayden. "Um, remind me again. Which one is it?"

He stepped into the room, toward the bank of televisions that ran from one end of the white wall, to the other. "The one about what I want to grow up to be." He beamed at the guard again. "Dennis's been telling me all about what it takes to be a security guard, and—" He shot us a "catch my drift" look, "—he's been letting me look at old camera footage as part of my research."

I blinked. Man, this kid had skills.

"Really?" asked Allison.

"Technically," said Dennis, "I need head office to clear the request, but Hayden's not going to use any footage, and besides—" His chest puffed out. "Part of being a security guard is making snap decisions. Knowing when to get help and when to do it on your own."

"We were just getting to last Friday's footage." Hayden turned to Dennis. "One of my friends was here and it would be so cool to see him. He says he sunk all his balls at pool, but I don't believe it."

Dennis chuckled. "Okay, let's see what we can find."

Hayden jumped on a chair covered with blue cloth. Its wheels spun with the force of his action and the chair slid toward Allison.

She caught it.

He scooted over and patted the spot beside him. "Come on, share."

She glanced at me.

"I'll stand."

She sat beside Hayden.

"Let's call it up," said Dennis. He tapped at his keyboard and launched into a lesson about the commands to use, how to request images by date or time, and the importance of having up-to-date software. "There we are. Friday, around three-thirty. Now, you said your friend was playing pool?"

Hayden nodded.

Alison bent over her phone.

The *clack-clack* of typing filled the room, and a split second after he finished, the image of the pool tables popped on the middle television screen.

We leaned forward, scanning the video to find Sal.

"There!" Allison pointed to the left part of the television.

Hayden and I squinted, and leaned closer.

"Can you zoom on him?" She asked Dennis.

The guard nodded. More keyboard-tapping . The image wasn't great and the camera angle was high but at least we could see what was going on.

"It's the best we can do," said Dennis. "We're mostly concerned with fights or kids going missing, so the cameras are set for wide-angles and group shots."

"No, it's fine," I said.

We watched the footage for a couple of minutes. Sal broke the balls, then sunk three. The fourth bounced off another ball and rolled alongside the rails.

"Well," Dennis chuckled. "I guess we just proved him a loser." He went to shut down the video.

"No!" We yelled it at the same time.

He turned, startled, his eyes wide, his mouth open.

"Sorry," I said. "Sal said it wasn't the first game, but I can't remember if it was the second or third."

"Oh." Dennis didn't look totally convinced, or happy at having had three kids yelling at him. "But we should shut this down. My shift is over in a couple of minutes. If another guard comes in and finds you here, I could get in trouble."

"Could you just speed up the tape?" asked Allison. "If you fast-forward the footage, we'll be able to see what happened, and you won't get in trouble."

We waited.

He looked at the clock then stared at the screen. "Okay—"

I let out my breath.

"—but we'll have to hurry it up."

We nodded.

He typed in the command.

I stared at the screen, not blinking in case I missed something. My eyes started to water, then throb. I blinked really fast, then went back to watching. But

Dennis had set up the video to go *really* fast and it was hard to see faces or catch what was really going on.

One of the kids went to Sal, asked him something. Sal set down his pool cue and went to his jacket. He pulled out a note, handed it to the kid. The kid moved off, and Sal took out his notebook and recorded the sale.

"So, he still had it," Allison whispered.

Sal set his coat back on the stool and picked up his pool cue. A couple of minutes later, a waitress came by with a tray of pizza and pop. Christopher pulled some money out of his back pocket and paid her. A group of kids moved in front of table. They blocked our view and the tape was going too fast for me to recognize anyone. Plus, I think they were using old technology because there was a white spot in the middle of the screen.

When they were gone, Sal was eating pizza and drinking his cola. The video continued to scroll until Sal set his pool cue down for the last time. He picked his coat up off the floor and then left.

Silence came into the security room.

"I guess you were right." Allison turned to Dennis. "He was lying." She stood. "We should go." She stuck her hand out. "Thanks for all your help."

He shook her hand and nodded. "Good luck with your project, Hayden."

We left. "That was a waste," said Hayden.

The door closed behind us just as a security guard came around the corner. He frowned. "You kids need something?"

I shook my head. "No, thanks."

"Then you should go," he said. "This area really isn't for anyone who doesn't have business with security."

I nodded and led my team out of the Game-O-Rama.

"I'm starving," said Hayden.

"Me, too," agreed Alison. She jerked her head toward the Burger Giant across the street. "Let's go eat. We'll bill it to Sal as an expense."

"Sounds good," I said, not really paying attention and looking at the doors of the Game-O-Rama.

"I should go," said Hayden. "My mom doesn't like me eating junk food."

"Well, we'll catch you up tomorrow, k?" said Allison.

He nodded. "Yeah." His mouth twisted to the side. "I'm sorry I couldn't be more helpful. I thought if we could see the video—I didn't think Dennis would run it so fast."

Allison looked at me, with that weird look girls give you when they're trying to silently give you a message. I had no idea what she was trying to say.

She sighed and rolled her eyes. "You did great." She put her hand on his shoulder.

He nodded and left.

We crossed the street and went into the restaurant. The place was mostly empty. We put in our orders. I wanted a burger, chocolate shake, and fries. Allison took a veggie-burger with onion rings and a cola.

I took the tray and found a corner booth.

We dug in. Junk food always tastes good, but after a day of work, it tastes *extra good.*

"Today went pretty good, didn't it?" asked Allison. "We really worked as a team."

"Hmm? Yeah." I took another bite of my burger and washed it down with a swig of chocolate milkshake. "There was something weird with the video—"

"Especially Hayden."

It took me a minute to process what she was saying. Then it took me another minute not to be irritated. I mean he'd done his job. "I guess."

"You guess? That was crazy smart thinking! He had that guard willing to show us anything."

68

Now, irritation turned to annoyance. She was vying for compliments and I was trying to solve the case. Girls. "He should have told us what he was going to do."

There was a pause. Electricity charged the air, then Allison launched into me.

"Are you for real?"

Her sharp words and the way she screeched them startled me so much, I spilled some fries onto the tray.

"Seriously—" Her voice went higher. "You're self-centered and self-involved—"

"*What!*"

"You don't think of anyone else but yourself."

I wanted to throw her burger across the restaurant. I wanted to yell and say things that would get me grounded for a month. Instead, I took a deep breath that made my lungs burn and said, "If that was true, I'd never have hired you or Hayden."

"You didn't *hire* us," she said bitterly. "We work for free, remember?"

Nuts. She got me.

"And you only use us because it makes your job easier."

"Well, I wouldn't have hired—given you a chance—if it made my job harder. That would be stupid."

"You'd know all about that," she muttered.

"I don't think I'm the one with the problem," I said, my voice hard. "I think it's you."

"You're right," she said.

That shocked me into silence.

"I'm an idiot for thinking you could do anything but think of yourself."

It took me thirty seconds of strained silence for me to figure out she'd just insulted me. I opened my mouth to rebut, but she jumped in.

"Hayden works his butt off for you. The kid—though I can't figure out why—thinks you're the best thing, ever. He even dresses like you, Billy."

I heard the desperation in her voice, but I couldn't figure out what she was trying to say. "So?"

"So—so don't you think he'd appreciate a 'good job, buddy' or 'nice going.' Geez, Billy, he got us security footage and helped us figure out that someone's after Sal. Without him, we'd still think it was a lost notebook." She took a breath. "You don't appreciate stuff we do."

"That's not true. I said thanks."

"Yah?" She challenged me. "When?"

"Uh—"

"That's what I thought."

"No, it was yesterday at lunch. I said nice work."

"You said, 'don't forget the ketchup.'"

Double nuts. She was right.

"You know what," she said, her voice weary, like we'd just gone ten rounds. "Just forget I said anything. Go back to the video. What bugged you?"

I took a bite of my fry, but it had no taste. Was she right? Had I never said thanks or good job? "I'm sure I've said thanks—"

"Just forget it." She shook her head. "I don't want to talk about it anymore."

"Then why did you bring it up?"

She shot me a glare so full of heat, it made my skin burn. "I said forget it."

I took the hint and went back to eating the burger.

"The coat on the ground," I said.

"What's so weird about that?"

"It was on the stool."

She shrugged. "So, it fell off."

I swallowed another bite of burger. "Doesn't make sense. It sat on the stool the whole time. Then suddenly, it was on the ground." I squeezed my eyes shut. "I just can't remember when it fell."

Allison's chewing slowed, then stopped. "It was just about the time the group of girls blocked the

70

camera."

"It would explain how it ended up on the floor and why no one turned it in to the Lost and Found."

"Good point." She paused. "So who would want to steal his book?"

"That's a long list."

"Someone who hated him, or was afraid of him."

"That's an even longer list."

"We'll have to talk to him," she said, "and get some names."

I grunted my agreement, my mind already compiling a list of kids Sal had ripped off, bullied, or screwed over. But like I'd said, it was a long list. This case was going to take forever to solve.

The next morning, I was at the school extra early. It was getting too cold to keep meeting in the tunnel. I didn't think Allison was right. I was sure I'd said "thanks," but just in case, I wanted to surprise the team by getting us permission to meet in the library. It would be warm and private, and maybe it would show them that they mattered to me.

Part of me didn't like this. I felt like I was being forced into doing something nice. But another—bigger—part of me liked the idea of seeing their smiles, and of doing something that they didn't expect. After changing into my sneakers, I went to find Mrs. Larson. I figured I could convince her to let us use the library. She seemed the type of teacher who liked to "encourage young minds."

This early, the school was quiet, sleepy. The custodial staff only had half the lights on, which left some of the hallways dark and in shadow. I went toward the staff room. The rubber from my sneakers squeaked on the floor and the sound echoed off the cement walls. I rounded the corner and almost slammed into Mrs. Smith.

She squinted and peered down her hooked nose. Fumbling, she grasped her glasses from the chain around her neck and shoved them on. Coffee sloshed from the cup she held and splashed against her worn, yellow sweater. She focused on me. Her gaze went from peering to glaring. "Vale. I might have known. What are you doing here?"

She leaned closer and the smell of garlic and coffee made my nose burn. "I wanted to see Mrs. Larson."

"Eh? What for?"

She brought her face close to mine. Stains left by her coffee gave her teeth a yellow glow and turned her breath sour.

"What are you playing at?"

"Nothing. I just wanted to see Mrs. Larson." I cleared my throat and stepped back. "Is she here, yet?"

Mrs. Smith kept staring.

I shifted. A Private Investigator isn't supposed to scare easy. We're supposed to look danger in the eye and laugh. But looking at Mrs. Smith, I couldn't summon a laugh. I couldn't even force a chortle.

"I saw you with Sal," she said. "What's going on?"

I said nothing.

"I'm giving you a chance to come clean, Vale. Everyone knows that kid's Trouble, with a capital 'T.'" She straightened. "You're trouble, with a lowercase 't.'" She took a long, slow sip of her coffee and stared at me from over its rim. "Whatever he's asked you to do, I wouldn't do it. He's on the radar with the principal and the superintendent."

I frowned. She was giving me a warning, but it was more than that. Mrs. Smith was giving me a *helpful* warning. Something was weird. The only thing she'd help me do is get a two-week stay in social skills. She kept slurping her coffee, and kept staring at me. Mrs. Smith stood like she had all the time in the world, but I saw the light in her beady eyes. She was waiting for me to break, to cave in and tell her about the case.

"I should go and see Mrs. Larson," I said, moved

around her.

"I know what you're looking for," she called after me.

I skidded to a stop and turned around.

She looked at me like a shark looks at fish. "Some things are better left lost than found, Vale. Remember that."

She followed me to the staff room.

I found Mrs. Larson by the photocopier. When I called her name, she turned and blinked fast. I squinted and stared at her eyes.

She blushed and swiped her cheeks.

Yep. I'd caught a teacher crying.

She forced a smile. "Billy. I'm glad I found you."

"Actually, I found—"

"I want to talk to you about the Artist Night."

I swallowed my groan, but my feelings must have shown because her face squashed together like I'd said a bad word.

"Don't worry," she said stiffly. "We—" She glanced at Mrs. Smith. "—had to cancel the event. *Some people* don't think there's enough money in the budget."

"Downtown's been very clear about the money, Trudy," said Mrs. Smith. "We can't be spending willy-nilly—"

"It's the arts." Mrs. Larson's tone was bitter. "Kids need a creative outlet—"

"There are rules." Mrs. Smith stared her down. "And I follow them."

I didn't have a clue what they were talking about. The way they talked to each other was like my mom and dad when they were fighting but trying to pretend they weren't fighting. I took a step back. "Um, I just wanted to know if I could use the library in the mornings."

Both teachers stopped talking and stared at me. I got a funny feeling in my stomach. They were going to keep fighting, but now, they were going to fight over me.

Sure enough, Mrs. Smith said, "No. No way."

"You don't even know what he wants," snapped Mrs. Larson. She smiled and asked, "What are you trying to do?"

Even though Mrs. Smith tried to get her to say "no," it only took a couple of minutes for me to convince her to let my team use the library. I went back outside to wait for Allison and Hayden. As I crossed the gravel, I saw a gold Mercedes pull up to the front doors. Hayden climbed out of the back seat. His mom stepped out of the passenger side.

I couldn't hear what was going on, but I saw the look on Hayden's face: miserable. His mom tugged at his jacket, fussed over his hair. He just stood there, like a robot: stiff, unmoving. His dad got out of the driver's seat. He said something to the mom—something not good, if I could judge by the way his face twisted and his eyebrows pulled down.

Her head snapped back, her hair swung out. She said something, followed it with a cutting motion with her hand. Hayden's dad looked more than angry. He looked furious. He got back into the car and slammed the door. Hard.

Hayden's mom kept smoothing his hair, buttoning and unbuttoning his coat. She pushed her face close to his. He turned from her. Then he shrugged out of her grip and moved away.

I heard her voice, faint and distant, calling, "Hayden, wait!" She took a few steps after him.

He kept walking.

His dad laid on the horn.

His mom did something with her finger that would get me grounded, for sure. Then she stomped to the car, got in, and slammed the door harder than the dad had. The tires pealed and the car lurched away.

I scrambled back to the school. Keeping the door

open a crack, I watched the bike racks. Once Hayden was there, I counted to ten, then went outside.

He saw me and forced a smile.

"Hey," I said.

"Hey."

"How are you?"

He blinked, then he frowned. Then he glowered. "Why?"

I took a step back. "I'm just asking."

"You never ask."

"Okay, okay." I held my hands up. "I'm sorry."

"Why are you asking?"

"What? Look, just forget it."

"No." He was off the bars and glaring up at me. "Why did you ask?" He stopped and looked back, toward the spot his parents had dropped him off. "Did you see something?"

"What—" Nuts. What was I going to say? I stared at his upturned face. Anger turned his cheeks red and made his freckles pop. No way was I going to tell him about seeing his folks fighting. I decided to go with another truth. "Look, Allison said I wasn't paying enough attention to you guys. So, I'm paying attention, all right? Geez."

He blinked. Then he blinked again and the tight lines of his body softened. He unclenched his fists. "Okay, fine."

I stepped on the bar and leaned against the railing.

We didn't say anything until Allison arrived a few minutes later. She locked up her bike and pulled a small blanket out of her backpack. "I thought we might share," she said. "It's cold and slippery in the tunnel."

"We won't need it," I said.

Her eyes narrowed into reptilian slits. "Why? You decided to go back to being the lone detective?"

It took a lot of effort not to grin like an idiot and give away my surprise. "Come on. I'll show you." I took them inside and led them down the hall.

75

"I don't like this," said Hayden, plucking at my jacket sleeve. "I saw Mrs. Smith's car in the lot. If she catches us, we're dead meat."

"No, we're not," I said as I stepped into the library. "I talked to Mrs. Larson. We have permission to meet in the library every morning until ten minutes before the bell. Then we have to go outside."

Allison's eyes widened. "Are you serious?"

I nodded. "She thinks the detective agency is good 'extracurricular activity.' So, she's letting us use the library. Mrs. Smith knows but since we have permission, she can't do anything."

Allison looked impressed. So did Hayden. More than that, they looked proud. Of me. Warmth dropped in my stomach and spread out, like a pebble tossed into a pond. I realized, then, how much it had mattered to me that they care, that they were impressed.

"So?" I asked, my tone gruff. "We gonna work or just stare at each other?"

Allison smiled and moving to a scarred pressboard table, tossed her backpack on the top. "So, yesterday, when Dennis was showing us the video, I took the opportunity to record it on my phone."

"Seriously!" I grinned. "Awesome."

She blushed. "Thanks. I downloaded it to my computer and I'm running a program to slow down the footage and clear up the video. It should be done by tonight and then we'll have a better idea of who was there at the Game-O-Rama yesterday. Until then, I've been thinking—" She dumped out a bunch of papers.

Hayden took a seat beside her.

I took the spot opposite and spread her notes across the square surface.

"—we need to put together a list of kids who had it out for Sal."

"That's the whole school," said Hayden. "Hardly anyone likes him. I heard he'll give you candy or excuse notes on loan, and then charge you extra."

76

I nodded. "It's true. Usually his parent notes are a buck, but I heard Madison Lowman took one on a loan. He said she could pay him back in a week, but then he made her pay four dollars for it."

"That's not all." Allison pulled out a red-coloured sheet from the pile. "Junnie Lee couldn't pay back all she owed for the candy he supplied, so he took her iPod."

Hayden shook his head. "An iPod for some dumb candy? I can't believe it."

"Believe it," I said. "Sal uses Ky and Christopher to do all his dirty work. Trust me, when you have those guys on either side of you, losing a music player isn't as bad as losing your teeth."

"This is a list of all the kids who didn't just hate him. They *despised* him." She shook the paper.

I took it from her and scanned the names. "Big list."

"It's ranked with the kids who had the biggest motive on the top."

I grunted. "Okay. Let's split this up—" I was going to take the top five names, the most likely candidates. Then I remembered what Allison had said, about how I only thought of myself and personal glory. "Allison, you take numbers one to five. Hayden, you're six to ten. I'll take numbers eleven to fifteen, and I'll talk to Sal. Maybe he knows someone who should be on the list."

****

"People love me," he said as he reached into a plastic container and tossed a handful of sunflower seeds at a group of pigeons.

I pulled my jacket closer and pressed myself against the brick wall of the school. "Are you kidding?"

"I provide a valuable service." He nodded toward the alcove, where four tech kids huddled together. The light from their game players lit their faces in a pale,

77

blue glow. One kid stood as a lookout, because that stuff wasn't allowed on school property. "You think they could function without the necessary sugar rush? Of course not. They're scores would suffer and then where would they be? Gaming's all they got."

I frowned and matched his pace has he headed toward his "office"—the grove of trees that bordered school property. "Just because they buy your junk doesn't mean they like you. They're indebted to you, afraid of you, but like you? Give me a break. You don't have any friends."

His head snapped to the side and his beady eyes went dark with contempt. "I got Ky and Christopher. That's two more than you have."

I froze. "I have lots of friends."

He gave me a pitying look. "You have clients. Not friends."

"I have Allison and Hayden—"

"They're not friends. They're your competition—you just don't know it, yet." His lips twisted down. "You did it all wrong. You never should have taken them on. Now, they'll learn everything, branch out, and take your business."

"They will not!" The words came out hot and hard. "They're my—"

"Your what?" He sneered. "Your friends? If you were smart, you would have done it like me. Ky and Christopher help—they distribute and keep the kids in line, but they don't know about ordering inventory or nothing. That's how you keep your hold on the market, Vale."

"This isn't about me," I ground the words out. "This is about you, and kids who have motive to destroy your business."

"No one's got motive. We're friends."

Man, this guy was repetitive. "You set Ky and Christopher on Harold when he couldn't pay his tab. The kid was so freaked out, he took off running, tripped over a hole in the asphalt, and broke his ankle. His folks found out about the forged notes and him skipping school to play at Game-O-Rama, and grounded him for the rest of the year. He's just one example of—"

"My business isn't like yours, Vale. Say your sweet co-worker Allison takes all your clients—"

"—she'd *never* do that—"

"—and runs the business into the ground. So what? A bunch of kids have some creative lying to do when they have to explain why they lost their cell phone. But me? My clients are dependent." He stuffed his hands into the pocket of his jeans. "You know what sugar does to the human body? Or all those sweet, tangy combinations of taste in fast food?"

"Yeah. It makes you fat."

"More than that—the stuff's addictive. It changes how your brain's wired. My clients don't just want my services, Vale." A slimy smile crawled across his face. "They *need* it." He pulled a toothpick out and stuck it in his mouth. "They depend on me. None of them would turn on me."

I did a quick turn and raced to find Allison.

"He's a dealer," I gasped when I finally found her by the teacher's parking lot. "Sal's a dealer."

She gave me a trademark "Duh" look. "I know."

"No, no—" I hunched over, clutched my chest and tried to get in some air. "A drug dealer."

Her eyes went wide. "What kind of drugs?"

"Sugar and salt."

She got that look again, the one that said I was the biggest idiot in school. "Billy, those aren't drugs."

"That's not what he said. He said that the way junk food and fast food's made, it's addictive. It re-wires the brain." I straightened. "We can't keep him as a client. We can't help a drug dealer."

She leaned against the metal railing, blew on her fingers and rubbed them together. "Look, are you sure that's what he said?"

I nodded.

Her mouth pulled to the left. "Let me do some research during reading time—"

The bell rang.

"—we'll meet up in the tunnel at recess, and I'll tell you what I found."

It was a tense two hours until recess came. As soon as I got out of the classroom, I dashed to our meeting spot. "So?" I asked as she came into the tunnel.

"So..." She sighed. "He was right." Allison reached into the sleeve of her jacket and pulled a sheaf of papers. "I did some research during free-reading." She looked up. "Are you sure you want to hear this?"

*No.* My lungs tightened and my stomach cramped. "Yes."

"Okay, there was an article in a magazine called 'Nature Neuroscience' that says junk food has the same effect on the brain as heroine."

"Heroine? *Heroine?*" Oh, man. It was worse than I thought. "We've been helping a guy who's basically feeding kids the burger and chip version of heroine." I groaned and slumped against the tunnel. "My mom's gonna kill me."

Allison stuck the papers back into the sleeve of her coat. "The sooner we solve the case, the sooner we're done with him."

My eyes widened. "The sooner—are you crazy? We can't keep him as a client!"

"Billy—"

She was using her teacher voice.

"—we took him on *and* he paid—"

"We'll give him the money back."

She shook her head and her hair curled around her face. "No. We keep him as a client."

Now, it was my turn to shake my head. "You really are crazy."

She sighed. "Look, being a detective isn't that

different from being a lawyer. Sometimes, your clients stink, but you still have to do the right thing and finish the job."

"But we're not lawyers. We're detectives. Why don't we drop him?"

She took off her glasses and squeezed her eyes shut. "Because sugar and salt aren't illegal. Plus, in the right amounts, you actually need that stuff. Anyway, my mom says everyone deserves representation, and if lawyers only took cases of 'good' people, we'd all be in trouble."

My eyebrows pulled together. "My mom's a mechanic. We talk about oil changes, block heaters, and making sure clients pay for work."

Allison grinned. "Yeah, my mom says the same thing—about clients, I mean."

The tunnel went silent and I watched her for a minute. I took a breath and felt the tight feeling leave my lungs. I turned away.

"You okay?"

"Yeah." My voice sounded gruff. "I just—I…I don't want us to fight about this."

She nodded and turned her gaze to the window. "Me, too."

I couldn't bring myself to say the rest: that she was my friend—the first I'd ever really had, and the idea of us fighting made me feel sick.

She sighed. "If I drop this case, my mom will kill me."

I snorted. "If I keep it, *my* mom will kill me."

"Compromise," she said. "I'll take this case."

"Wh-what?" My mouth went dry.

She turned and smiled. "I'll run this one, with Hayden. That way, your mom can't get mad at you, and my mom won't give me the run-down of the legal system and civil rights." Her smile widened. "What do you think?"

*I think Sal was right.* Ice-cold spread from my

insides out.

Her smile dimmed. "Listen, it's just a suggestion. You don't have to—"

"No," I said, not sure if I was talking to her or that stupid thought in my brain. I forced a smile. Allison was my friend and she was nothing like Sal implied. "I'll stay—" I swallowed hard. "You're right. I mean, I don't like it, but you're right. We took the case, we should finish it."

She nodded and the skin around her face relaxed. "Good. I mean, I would have done it for you, but let's face facts. Sal's comfortable with you. Even with Hayden, it would have been brutal without you." She grinned. "That's why you're the chief."

*See? I told myself. She's your friend. She's not going to take away your business. Sal's totally wrong.*

Maybe.

Probably.

But I couldn't shake the feeling like I'd stared into the agency's future—and it didn't include me.

\*\*\*\*

That night Allison phoned. "Remember the video from Game-O-Rama?"

"Yeah."

"Well, I thought I'd have to a bunch of extra work because of that white spot in the camera."

"Yeah, I saw that, too. Old technology, I guess."

"That's what I figured, but I was wrong. Turns out it was someone's coat. You know anyone who wears sequined jacket?"

My skin went hot then cold. "Tomorrow's Saturday. Meet me at the Brahna Yoga Studio at ten o'clock. You just found our culprit."

"Really?" Pleasure made her voice jump an octave.

"Really. You're talking about Mikhail Pinkerton. He used to be the dealer for MacDonald until Sal ran him out of business. There's no one with a better motive for getting back at Sal. Tomorrow, okay?"

82

"Okay."

I hung up the phone and headed downstairs for a bowl of popcorn—the unsalted kind. Nothing like solving a case to make a kid want to celebrate, but what Allison had told me about junk food freaked me out. I was going to make sure I cut back because I definitely didn't want my brain re-wired!

****

"You guys are nuts." Mikhail sat on a blue yoga mat and crossed his legs, lotus-position.

"Nuts like a lima bean," muttered Allison. She dropped beside him and squinted against the light streaming through the windows of his mother's yoga studio. "We have video of you at the Game-O-Rama."

"Of course I'm there." He tossed his shaggy, brown hair to the side and closed his eyes. "I find the Game-O-Rmaa good for restoring my chi." His right eye popped open. "Chi—that's your spiritual balance and connection to the universe."

"I know what 'chi' is." Allison nose wrinkled in disgust and she shot me a "how dumb does he think we are" look.

I sneered in agreement, although I was happy he'd defined the word. I didn't have a clue what it meant.

"Don't you think it's weird that you're at the Game-O-Rama on the day Sal loses his record book? He'll be ruined."

Mikhail snorted, then quickly covered it with some kind of yoga chant. He closed his eyes. "Yoga teaches to let go of strife and forgive." Both eyes popped open. "But it couldn't happen to a more deserving guy."

"It would have been great payback," I said. "Take his book, do to him what he did to you."

Mikhail sighed and stood. Adjusting the waistband of his grey jogging pants, he said, "Look, I'll admit, there's no love lost between us, but I wouldn't have done it. Bad karma."

"Bad—"

"It means if I'd done anything bad to him, it would have bitten me on the butt, one way or another."

"I know that—"

"Besides, I got a good thing going with my mom's studio." He leaned in. "People may pay a lot of money for junk food, but it's *insane* what they'll pay for organic, earth friendly stuff. Do you know how much I can charge for bottled water?" He shook his head. "It's crazy. I'm making way more money doing this."

He grinned, but his smile looked wild, creepy.

"No one would let me sell chocolate because it's junk food, but sell a couple of granola bars at double the price it cost me to buy it?" He shook his head. "That's okay because it's a healthy alternative." He rubbed his hands together. "I've been talking to the principal and I figure if I play my cards right, I can convince him that I should be the only kid who gets to supply the school."

Allison jerked back. "That's a monopoly—"

He laughed. "Monopoly's not just a board game." The smile faded from his face. "Look, I'm sorry about what happened to Sal, but I didn't do anything."

"I can prove it."

"I'd like to see you try," he sneered.

Allison whipped out her cell phone and called up the video. In digital clarity was the proof: Mikhail going into Sal's jacket and taking the notebook.

The blood emptied from Mikhail's face and his eyes went wide. "Where did you get that?"

"I'm—*we're* the best detectives in the school," I said. "So, the question is this: do we give a copy of this to Sal?"

"Look…you can't show him this. That kid's crazy. He'll beat me up or worse!"

Allison slipped her phone back into her pocket. "Why did you do it? You said you were doing better selling the organic stuff."

He groaned and flopped on the mat. "I was—I am.

But I was there on Friday and when I saw him…I don't know. It's like all the anger came back. He stole my business and I knew without the book, he'd be ruined." He took a breath. "I know I should be sorry, but I'm not. I can't stand that kid." He swivelled his head toward me. "But if my mom finds out about this, she'll be really mad. Plus Sal—" He covered his face with his hands. "I'm going to be grounded forever *and* I'll have two black eyes and missing teeth."

Allison and I exchanged glances and this time, I knew what she was saying.

"Give me the book," I sighed. "We'll keep you out of it."

My partner beamed at me.

He spread his fingers and looked at us. "Seriously."

"On one condition," said Allison. "You drop the price of your product."

His face scrunched together like she'd shoved two lemons in his mouth.

She shrugged. "Take it or leave it."

He stood and went to his gym bag. Pulling out Sal's black book, he said, "I'll take it."

I put the book in my back pocket and we left the studio. "Good work, partner."

Allison grinned. "We should tell Sal."

I nodded. "Do you have his phone number?"

She nodded and dialed it.

I took the phone and told him the notebook had been found.

"Found?" He asked. "No one took it?"

"Of course someone took it," I said, "How else would it have ended up back to us?"

"No, I meant—" He sighed. "Never mind. Where can I meet you?"

"West Edmonton Mall," I said. "And you can pay us the money you owe."

"Okay. See you in fifteen minutes." He hung up.

I handed the phone back to Allison. Then I

85

reached into my jacket and pulled out three loonies. "Here. Your share of the profit."

"Really?"

I nodded. "You and Hayden aren't just volunteers, anymore. I'll give him his share tomorrow."

She blinked really fast and smiled. "Billy—"

I turned away, embarrassed. "We should call Hayden. Celebrate our victory."

She nodded. "I agree. How do you want to celebrate?"

"I'd really like a slush, but maybe a fruit smoothie's a better idea."

"The mall's got a Happy Juice."

"Sounds like a good decision...partner."

She punched me on the shoulder. Then she gave me a soft look and said, "Thanks, Billy."

## The Case of Enigmatic Envelope

On Monday morning, when we came into the library, we found the envelope. It was crisp, white and lay in the middle of the table. Allison scooped it up, then handed it to me.

"It has your name on it," she said. "Looks like a case."

Thank goodness. For the past two weeks, things hadn't been very busy. I shrugged out of my backpack and coat, and sat down. The person had printed my name in black felt. Each letter was perfect. Too perfect. I squinted, trying to see if it was really as perfect as it seemed.

Hayden sighed. "Just open it."

"A detective checks out all the clues," I said.

Allison nodded. "That's what Lucas St. Cloud says, too."

Normally, I'd roll my eyes. She was always quoting from Dreamy McCloud's dumb *How to Be a Detective* book, but this time, she and the Cloud were right. "The person used a computer to print my name. Look, you can see the marks the printer made on the envelope. But then, the person used a felt marker to trace over my name. If you hold it to the light—"

Hayden held out his hand and I gave him the envelope.

"—you can see the ink of the pen and the printer don't match up. The ink must be running dry because the 'y' is missing its tail."

"So?" asked Allison.

"I don't know," I admitted. "Maybe they're trying to cover their tracks."

Allison's mouth twisted to the side. She frowned.

"Maybe." Then she grinned. "A secret client. Cool!"

"Okay." Hayden gave me the envelope. "Now, can we open it up?"

Reaching into my backpack, I took out a pencil. Then I slid it into the flap of the envelope and carefully pried it open.

"Hurry up, Billy," he said. "I'll be in grade six by the time you're done."

Lately, Hayden had been extra grouchy. Allison said it was obvious that his parents were still fighting and we should be patient. I had agreed, but sometimes he was really snarky and it was starting to bother me.

"Give me a break," I said. "We've got to do this right. It's weird to have someone just drop a note on the table. We need to go slow and log everything."

He rolled his eyes.

I glanced at Allison, but she shook her head, so I kept my mouth shut. Instead, I finished opening the envelope and using the pencil, pulled the letter out. Allison handed me another pencil and I used it to unfold the paper.

The person had typed out their note. In big, black letters it said, "I AM BEING BLACKMAILED. SECRECY IS OF VITAL IMPORTANCE. IF YOU WILL TAKE MY CASE, THEN WRITE "YES" ON THIS PAPER. THERE IS A BOOK ON THE TABLE AT THE BACK OF THE ROOM. IT IS CALLED "HOW TO WATCH PAINT DRY—A BEGINNER'S GUIDE" BY HANS MEET. PUT THE ENVELOPE IN BETWEEN THE BOOK COVER AND THE FIRST PAGE. I WILL USE THE BOOK TO CONTACT YOU."

Allison peered over my shoulder. "That's not a lot of information."

"Blackmail," said Hayden. "What's that all about?"

"It means that our client—let's call them "Al"— did something he doesn't want anyone to know about. Now, someone else—let's call them "Hank"—has threatened Al. If Al doesn't pay or do what Hank says, then Hank's going to tell everyone about this thing that Al did." Allison leaned back. "That's blackmail."

Hayden shot her an annoyed look. "I know what blackmail means. I meant, in a school like MacDonald, what kind of secret is so bad a kid doesn't want anyone to know?"

"There's lots of secrets," I said. "Maybe they still wet the bed or they failed kindergarten. Maybe they live in a shelter—"

"—or their parents are fighting and they don't want anyone to know," finished Allison.

Hayden's skin turned red, starting at his neck and ending at his forehead. "We should take the case," he mumbled.

I nodded. Using the pencil, I wrote "yes" in block letters. Then I signed my name and handed the pencil to Allison and Hayden, so they could sign their names. When they were done, I folded the letter, put it back in the envelope.

We found the book and put the client's letter in between the pages.

"What happens, now?" asked Allison.

I shrugged. "We wait and see." I paused. "When do you have library class?"

"After lunch," said Allison.

"Just before lunch," said Hayden.

"Okay," I said. "I have it at two o'clock. So, this is what we'll do. Everyone takes a turn and checks the book. Whoever gets the letter, brings it to the rest of us. Deal?"

They nodded. The bell rang for classes to start and we went to our separate rooms.

At lunch, I did a quick check of the book. Our note was gone, but there wasn't anything new in its place. I left and met up with Hayden in the lunchroom.

"I got you a veggie-burger," he said, "celery sticks,

and a chocolate milk."

"Thanks." Ever since I'd found out about the effects of sugar and salt, I'd been trying to eat healthier. "I checked the book, but there wasn't anything."

He nodded. "I figured. There was nothing there when I looked."

I took a bite of my burger and wiped the mustard off my cheek. "It's driving me crazy. I'm dying to know who the kid is, and what the big secret is."

Before Hayden could answer, Sal came up to us. He waved the record book at us. "What gives?"

Hayden and I glanced at each other.

"I dunno," I said. "What gives?"

"There's a page missing."

"How do you know?"

His lip curled back. "Because it's my book. I know the weight and how it feels—there's a page missing."

I shrugged. "So? If you know your records so well, then just put back the information."

He shook his head and his hair fell across his forehead. "I don't—it's not like that. I haven't memorized every page of the book. But I know records from certain clients are missing." His eyes narrowed. "That's your fault."

"How?"

"You had my book" he said. "Now, there's stuff missing."

"And you think we took it?" Hayden's voice went high with surprise.

Sal yanked out a chair. Its metal legs screeched against the floor. He straddled the seat and glared at me. "I know how you feel about me and my business."

I rolled my eyes. "And you think I stole a page from your book?"

"Yeah, it would mess up my business. Hinder me."

"Sal, if I wanted to hinder you, I wouldn't have given you back your book."

"What's the big deal, anyway?" asked Hayden. "It's just a page."

"An *important* page." He shook his head and stood up. "The whole thing is just a mess. Find it, Vale."

I stretched my hand out. "Give me the fee."

Sal's face turned red, like he'd been holding his breath for too long. His eyes bulged out of his head. "*Pay* you! You lost the page. You find it or I'll ruin your business." He shoved the chair backwards, stalked off, and almost ran into Allison.

She sat down and put her notebook on the table. Jerking her head in Sal's direction, she asked, "What was that all about?"

I pushed my tray toward her and nodded toward the celery sticks.

"Thanks." She bit into one.

"Sal's just upset because a page is missing from his book and he's blaming us."

She stopped in mid-chew.

I straightened. "What?"

"Sal's in a sensitive business—do you think he's the one who sent us the note?"

Hayden's face scrunched together.

So did mine. "No. If he was missing a page, he'd just tell us. But—" I leaned forward. "—it would make sense if one of his clients was the one trying to hire us."

We glanced around the room. "Who do you think?"

"The athletic kids," said Hayden.

"The kids in the healthy-eating club," added Allison.

I sighed. "We won't know anything until we get another letter."

Allison took another celery stick. "Maybe it'll show up after lunch."

But it didn't. And it wasn't there after school. I left the library, dodging around Mrs. Smith, and went home. I wondered if we really had a new client, or if it had all been a prank.

The next day, I got my answer. In the book was another white envelope. I exhaled and felt the tightness in my chest loosen. "I wasn't sure they would contact us. I even waited until all the kids had left yesterday, but there was no note."

"I was worried, too," said Allison.

"Worry-schmurry." Hayden made a shooing gesture with his hands. "Hurry up and open it. What does it say?"

This time, I didn't bother with using pencils to open the envelope—though I did notice my name was printed with the inkjet ink. The "y" still looked like a "v." Hayden and Allison hovered over my shoulder.

"I am a client of Sal. Someone is blackmailing me. Find and stop him," read Allison.

Hayden grabbed the paper. "That's it?"

"They included a payment." I held up a five-dollar bill. "A big one."

Allison took the letter. "This is stupid. We don't have a name. We don't know what the blackmail is about. We don't know anything."

I grinned. "I know. It's the best case, ever."

"You must have skipped breakfast. Hunger is obviously making you crazy," said Allison.

"No, really. We're detectives. What's better than a case where we don't know anything?"

"A case where we have some information," said Hayden.

"We do. We know Sal's missing a page from his journal and we know our client is also one of his clients, which means—"

"Our client is probably one of the people on the missing page." Allison's eyes lit up.

"Exactly."

Hayden pursed his lips. "But Sal can't remember what's on the page."

"This is how we break it down," I said and leaned forward. "Let's say the blackmailer has the page and now our client—"

"Let's call him 'Bob,'" said Hayden. "It's easier than saying 'our client' all the time."

"Why Bob?" asked Allison. "Why can't it be a girl? Why not Rachel or Molly?"

"Bob is faster—it's just one syllable."

"So is 'Jill.'"

I raised my hands before they really got into it. "How about Bobbie? It can be either a boy's name or a girl's."

Allison and Hayden eyed each other, then nodded.

"Okay," I continued. "What would you do if someone found out you were going someplace you weren't supposed to go?"

"Stop going," said Hayden.

"Right," I said. "So we need to talk to Sal, see if anyone's dropped off."

Allison nodded. "That's one of McCloud's rules: look for changes in routine."

I rolled my eyes but didn't say anything.

We headed to Sal's spot by the trees, but he was no help.

"Since word got out about the missing page, my business is down," he said. He pulled the toothpick out of his mouth, inspected it. "Kids are scared. They think I can't protect their privacy. No one wants detention or an extra visit to the dentist." His lips turned down in a scowl. "I'm just getting by." He turned his glare on me. "What are you doing about *my* case? You're here, asking about some unknown client. What about me? What about following up on my page?"

"That's what we're doing," I said. "I think if we find your page, we can find out who's blackmailing our client."

"Well, find it and find it fast." He tossed the

toothpick on the ground.

"Hey!" Allison pointed to it. "Pick it up."

"Make me," he sneered.

"I'll tell one of the recess monitors," she said.

"Yeah?" He sneered and said in a smug tone, "That makes you a snitch. The big, bad detective lady has to run to the teachers for help."

Allison's face turned crimson. She grabbed Sal by the front of his coat, leaned in, and whispered something in his ear.

He tried to pull away.

She tightened her grip and kept whispering.

His eyes widened, then narrowed. "Aw, *geez.*" He pulled away from her. Shooting her a dirty look, he bent down and grabbed the toothpick. He pointed at me. "Keep her away from me, Vale. You and I talk or there's no talk." He shoved the toothpick in his pocket, jerked his head at Ky and Christopher. They stomped away.

"What did you say to him?" asked Hayden.

Allison watched Sal's retreating figure. "Do you really want to know?"

Hayden and I locked eyes.

"No," he said.

I held up my hands. "Me either."

"What, now?" she asked.

Truth was, I didn't know. I turned in a slow circle, hoping to catch an idea from my surroundings. Instead, I saw Mrs. Smith, staring at us. Her beady eyes were narrowed and she was muttering to herself.

She caught me watching. Slowly, she turned and walked away.

"Billy?"

"Uh—" I tilted my head toward Allison. "If Sal doesn't know, maybe his top clients have an idea. We know some of the kids who're always buying from him. Allison, you and I will go to them. We'll ask if they remember the kids who were around when they were getting candy or notes. That way, we can make up our own list."

She nodded.

"What about me?" asked Hayden.

"You watch Sal. Get a list going of who comes to him. Then, we can compare your names with ours."

"And the kids who aren't crossed off your list," he said, "are the kids who aren't going to him anymore."

"And in that list," I said, "has got to be Bobbie."

The next day, I let Allison take the lead on getting names. I had another task to do: tail Mrs. Smith. She'd been at the library and the playground. I had a feeling she knew something and it scratched at me like a wool sweater. At morning recess, I tried to follow her and see where she was going.

Unfortunately, she went into the teacher's room. Principal Lee caught me lurking by the door and kicked me out. Lunch was no better. Mrs. Smith ducked into the copy room and wouldn't come out. By the time school ended, I was tired and frustrated.

I met Allison and Hayden at the library, hoping they'd had better luck. But just like me, they'd struck out.

"It's no use," said Allison. "There are too many kids for us to figure out who's the one being blackmailed."

I kicked at the metal leg of the table. "There's got to be a way. Someone wrote us those notes."

"And they wrote us this one, too." Hayden handed me a white envelope. He jerked his thumb toward the back of the room. "I saw a piece of white sticking out of the paint book and thought I'd check."

I ripped open the paper and took out the letter. A five-dollar bill fluttered to the ground. "Stop wasting your time on teachers," I read. "Find out who's blackmailing me."

Allison's eyes went bright and she jerked upright.

"Our client was following you."

"Yeah," I said irritably. "Just what I need: a shadow."

"Don't you see?" She pulled on the sleeve of my sweater. "Our client is following you."

I pried her fingers off. "I got that."

"No—no, I mean—" She adjusted the red frames of her glasses. "We're trying to figure out who our client is. So, if they've been following you—"

I snapped my fingers. "Then we need to pay attention to who's around us."

"Exactly! Find out who's tailing you and we find our client."

Hayden sat in the chair next to me. "You should keep tailing Mrs. Smith. Bobbie was annoyed enough to write you a letter. For sure, they're going to follow you and see what you do."

I nodded. My ears twitched at the sound of someone singing.

"Mrs. Larson," said Hayden.

"Why is she singing?" I asked.

"Because the Artist Event is back."

I frowned. "I thought there wasn't money."

Allison shrugged. "All I heard was Mrs. Smith and Mrs. Larson got together and found the funds."

My frown deepened. Mrs. Smith had done something nice? That didn't sound like her. Mrs. Larson's singing grew louder. She came into the library, saw us, and beamed.

"I'm putting up posters for the event," she said. "Do you want to take one home?"

"Um, no that's okay," I said.

"Uh, yeah. I'm okay, too." Hayden slunk into his chair.

"I'll take one," said Allison and held her hand out.

Mrs. Larson handed her a page, then left our table.

I glanced at the poster. "Wow. Color and everything. They really must have found some money."

Allison nodded. "She's working really hard to put it together."

"She's going nuts," grumbled Hayden. "Yesterday, she was asking me to do a reading. I'm six! What am I going to read?"

Allison stood. "I'd go nuts, too. Can you imagine how hard she had to work to get old Smith to approve the event?"

"I'd rather have a year's detention." Hayden shuddered. "No one wants a fight with Mrs. Smith." He glanced at the clock and grimaced. "I have to go. My mom's going to be here in a couple of minutes to pick me up."

I stood. "We have a plan. Tomorrow, we'll finally catch a break."

The next day, I kept following Mrs. Smith. Allison tailed me—at a distance, so no one would catch on to our plan. At the end of school, we met at the library and compared notes.

"I made a list of the kids who followed you." She bent over the paper. Her glasses slid down the bridge of her nose. She pushed them up and looked at me.

"How big is the list?" I asked.

Her mouth pulled to the side. She held up the paper. It was blank.

I grabbed it and shot her a look of disbelief. "Are you kidding?"

She shook her head. "There were kids who were at the same location as you. Like, when you were in the lunchroom, Marta, Allen, and Josie were there. But none of them were there when you were at the science lab." She shrugged. "Whoever this kid is, they're really good at covering their tracks."

I sighed and rubbed my forehead. "Okay, thanks."

She stood. "I'm really sorry. Tomorrow, though, we'll figure it out."

I nodded.

She left.

I crumpled the paper and tossed it at the recycling can. It missed. I sighed. Man. I couldn't figure out who our client was, couldn't figure out who'd stolen Sal's paper, and I couldn't even get a ball into the basket. This day was sucking harder than my mom's new vacuum cleaner. As I stood and walked over to the recycling can, I glanced at the paint book. A sliver of white paper stuck out of its pages.

I jogged over to the book and pulled out the envelope. Tearing it open, I read, "What did I say? Forget the teacher. Find the blackmailer."

Something tickled my brain. There was a clue— more than that, there was an answer. It lurked in the back of my mind and scratched at my brain. I walked back to the recycling can, bent down, grabbed Allison's paper, and tossed it in. As I stood, the scratch feeling intensified. I went into the hallway and looked at the posters Mrs. Larson was putting up. Scanning the page, I read: "Artist Night on Tuesday—"

My gaze locked on the "y" in "Tuesday." Sure enough, it was missing a tail. My skin felt like I'd jumped into snow: cold and tingly. "Mrs. Larson—"

She beamed at me.

"—why is the 'y' missing its tail?"

"Because I'm old-fashioned." She leaned in and whispered, "There's an old typewriter in the staff room. I love using it to write notes. It's the sound of the keys." She straightened and shivered. "It's like music."

Blood raced through my veins. I felt hot and breathless. I knew who my client was. "Okay. Thanks."

"Are you going to participate in the Artist—"

"Um, I'll think about it." I raced down the hall, past the bulletin boards with the drawings of the kindergarten class, and headed toward room fifteen. When I saw the door, I skidded to a stop. I took a couple of seconds to catch my breath, then I headed into the dragon's den. "Working late?" I asked as I stepped inside.

Mrs. Smith sat at her desk and looked up when I asked the question. Her eyes narrowed into snake-like slits and her mouth pursed up like a prune. "Vale."

I didn't know how to do anything but tell her the truth. "You're the client," I said.

Her eyes narrowed further until I couldn't see her pupils. "Close the door."

I gulped. It was one thing to confront her with the door open. When it was closed, no one could hear me. Still, a detective's gotta do what a detective's gotta do. I shut the door.

"What are you talking about?" She clasped her hands together. Her gnarled fingers rubbed against each other.

"You're the client," I repeated. I walked toward her, pretended that my knees weren't wobbling and my stomach wasn't quaking.

"Prove it."

"Allison."

She frowned.

"Your first mistake was using the staffroom typewriter. It never prints the 'y' properly. Kids aren't allowed in the teacher's area."

"Not true. What about student secretaries?"

I nodded. "You're right, but it still narrowed down our list—only a certain amount of kids have permission to use that printer. But we were still thinking it was a kid." I took a breath. "Then you made your biggest mistake. You sent us the note telling us to stop talking to the teachers. Allison realized it meant our client was following us."

The papery skin of her face went white. Every wrinkle stood out.

"Allison followed me today, making notes on who was around me. But there was only one person who was with me all the time—"

"Me," she whispered.

I nodded. "And when you sent the second note, I knew it had to be you."

Mrs. Smith put her head in her hands. Her shoulders slumped. "I was desperate," she said, her voice dull. "I had to make sure you were on top of the case."

I shifted. My legs and stomach felt like they were full wriggling worms. I'd never seen Mrs. Smith beaten or unsure of herself. It was like finding out the earth was flat. "Why didn't you just ask me?"

She slowly raised her head. For a moment, she stared at me with her watery eyes. Then she snorted. Mrs. Smith got to her feet, but she did it at a snail's pace, moving as though her entire body hurt. "Right," she said. "*Ask* you. Just like that. As if we don't hate each other." She lifted her gaze. Her eyes were full of contempt. "You think I'd give you that kind of power?"

I held her gaze, stared right back at her, even though I was totally freaked. "We're here, right now," I said. "And you still need my help."

She blinked, fast and hard. Then she sank into her seat, like a balloon that had lost its air. "Here we are." Mrs. Smith bent her head.

Instinct told me not to say a word.

"You think it's easy?" Her voice was muffled.

I didn't know what she was talking about.

"You think it's easy?" she asked again. "You think this is how I thought my life as a teacher would be?" She lifted her head but she didn't look at me. Instead, she stared at the window. "When I first started teaching, kids used to bring apples and leave them on my desk. We had school nurses. Parents would come to assemblies. Now—" Her face squashed together as if she was in pain. "Now, there's not enough money for supplies, kids act like jerks, and the parents don't care."

Mrs. Smith turned and looked me right in the eye.

"My friend was almost fired because she failed a kid. He hadn't done the work. She thought sending him to a higher grade when he didn't know the material would do more harm than good. You know what his parents and the principal said? That not sending him would hurt his self-esteem." She hit the desk with her fist.

I jumped.

"He can't do the work! How will it help him to be in a class where he's the one always failing?" She shook her head and the fire in her eyes died. "Candy. Chocolate. It was the only thing that made me happy."

"Why didn't you just buy it at a store? Why did you get it from Sal?"

Her jaw tightened and she jerked her head to the side. "Because I wanted to be strong," she whispered. "Every morning, I'd say to myself, 'Jessie—'"

Huh. I never knew her first name.

She straightened her shoulders. "—today, you're going to do it. You're going to go to school and you're going to be sunshine." Her body collapsed in. "I used to be sunshine," she whispered. She sunk further into her seat. "Every day, I tried to be strong. Every day, I tried to bring the sun." She sighed, long and heavy. "And every day—" She took off her glasses and rubbed her eyes. "—every day it was a new disaster. The plumbing had to be fixed. Something was broken on the playground. We needed new balls for gym. The toner in the photocopier was spewing ink. Something was always going wrong and there was never enough money to fix it." She took a deep, shuddering breath. "Do you know how awful it is to stare at a sheet and have to decide between spending money for books or getting in aides to help students? Why should a school have to decide things like this? Why can't we have both?"

Mrs. Smith smiled. The expression on her face was wistful, like she was remembering days from long ago. "When I started—oh—we had round pencils for kids and books and crayons. Now, I have a broken-

101

down school and an ulcer. I went to Sal because I never leave the school property until the end of the day. I went to Sal because any heart I had—" Her voice cracked. "—was used up by morning recess and the only thing that got me through the day was a chocolate bar."

Her eyes turned glassy and she smiled at me. "But every night, *every night,* I promised myself that tomorrow would be better." She clenched her fist. "Now, someone's blackmailing me and I'm all alone in this." She sighed, and rocked back. "Alone, except for you." Her gaze held me. "What are you going to do? Laugh? Tell all your friends?" She snorted. "Bet I'll be a big joke on the playground tomorrow."

"No, ma'am. I took this job and I'm going to finish it."

She watched me. "And my identity?"

"I have to tell Allison and Hayden. They're the only ones who'll ever know."

Her lips squeezed together. "Good," she said, her voice gruff.

I jerked my thumb toward the door. "I gotta go. Find clues and stuff."

She nodded. "Good luck."

I left. For a moment, I just leaned against the wall. I felt sad for her, and it made me feel *really* weird. I'd always thought of Mrs. Smith as a monster, a dragon. But now I knew she could be hurt. It made her human but I wasn't sure how I felt about it or her. I sighed and pushing off the wall, headed down the quiet hallway. Deciding to go out the doors by the office, I hung a left at the gym. Mrs. Larson was standing by the wall, a clipboard in her hand. She smiled brightly at me.

"Billy!" She said. "Come, we're starting auditions for the talent portion of the Artist Night. Try out."

"No, I can't."

"Come on." She waved toward the entrance. "It'll be fun. We're going to have hot chocolate and popcorn."

"I really can't. I'm on a case."

Her smile turned into a grin. "Something juicy?"

I felt an instinctive urge to protect Mrs. Smith. "Not really," I said, trying to be casual about it.

Mrs. Larson must have picked up on my internal feelings, because her grin vanished. She took a couple steps toward me. Concern draped her face. "Are you okay? Is it a client? Is there some way I can help?"

"Uh, no." I glanced down the hallway, checking to see if Mrs. Smith had come out of her room. I didn't want her to find me with Mrs. Larson. I didn't want her to think I was gossiping.

Mrs. Larson followed my gaze. Her mouth went into an "o" shape. "Oh, it's Jessie—Mrs. Smith." She turned back to me. Her head cocked to the side. She put her hand on my shoulder. "You're a good kid to help her. It hasn't been easy." She gave me a gentle push. "Go, find the culprit."

Relief made my breath come out in a *whoosh.* "Thanks." I stepped away and jogged to the door.

Then I skidded to a stop.

*You're a good kid to help her. It hasn't been easy.* Mrs. Smith said that she was alone in this, except for me. So, how did Mrs. Larson know anything? I did a slow pivot and turned to face the teacher.

She stiffened.

We stood, staring at each other.

I'd expected it to be a kid, not a teacher. How the heck was I supposed to get an adult in trouble?

Mrs. Larson lifted her arm and pointed to the empty conference room. "Why don't we go in there?"

My mouth went dry.

"Billy?"

I nodded but it felt like cement, not blood, flowed in my veins.

She moved to the door, then looked back.

I swallowed and forced my legs to move. My feet

seemed to weigh a million pounds and the path to the door looked as though it was ten miles long, but I made it inside. I leaned against the wall.

Mrs. Larson set the clipboard on the table. "I gave myself away, didn't I?" she asked quietly.

"Mrs.—" My voice croaked. "Mrs. Smith didn't tell anybody."

She nodded slowly. Then she sank into her chair. Mrs. Larson put her head in her hands. "I'm not proud of what I did."

I took a breath. "How did you manage to get the paper?"

"I made Sal hang his coat up in the locker room. When the kids were at music, I took the book out and cut the section that had her name. I knew about her...problem. We all did." She pressed her lips together. "But we just ignored it, pretended we didn't know what she was doing in the grove."

"But why did you do this to her?"

"Because she made me mad." She twisted in her seat. Mrs. Larson's eyes sparked with light. "Because she never let me do anything fun with the kids and I was angry."

I thought for a minute. "Your blackmail was the Artist Night. You made her agree to the contest."

She nodded. "Not every kid is good at math and language arts. Some kids can sing, some can dance, and some are great at karate." She blinked fast. "Don't they deserve a chance to show everyone they're good at *something*?"

I moved into the center of the room, walked to the table, and sat in the chair. "But there wasn't money."

Mrs. Larson pressed her lips together. Her jaw trembled. "I know." She looked at me, her eyes wide. "I just did it to tick her off, to make her feel as helpless as I did. But when she agreed, I...I wanted to take the chance."

I took a deep breath and tried to stop the pounding

of my heart. "It was wrong," I said and clutched at the legs of the table. I knew I was right in telling her, but she was a teacher and I was just a kid.

She didn't say anything.

"Mrs. Larson? It was wrong."

"She was rude and mean to me."

"It was wrong."

"So was she."

I took a breath. "That doesn't make it right."

She dipped her head.

I stood. "I'm just a kid," I said. "I can't really do anything...I think you're a good teacher."

She looked up, smiled.

I saw the tears in her eyes. "I'm not going to tell Mrs. Smith until tomorrow morning. You have tonight to tell her, to come clean, and say you're sorry."

"But she—"

"It was still wrong, what you did."

"I know," she whispered. "I was just tired of—we needed the talent show—we could have found the money somewhere."

I shrugged. "That's not my place. I'm a detective and I'm a kid. It's the adults who have to decide those things."

She smiled. "You're a good kid, Billy." She took a deep breath and stood. "I'll talk to Jessie after the tryouts." She stuck out her hand. "I promise."

I shook her hand. Then I stepped out of the door and headed to the exit. I pulled my coat close to my body. It was cold and windy outside, but I wondered how much colder and lonely it was for the two women inside the school. They both wanted what was best for us kids, and they couldn't find a compromise between the two of them. It was hard to be a kid, but today, I'd learned it was even harder to be an adult. I stepped on to the pavement and headed home.

## The Case of the Missing Man

The next morning, when we met in the library, I told Allison and Hayden what happened.

"Do you think they'll work it out?" asked Allison.

Hayden scowled and crossed his arms. "They're adults. They should work it out."

Allison and I looked at each other.

"Uh—" She shifted in her seat and adjusted her glasses. "I was talking to Madison on the phone yesterday." Allison's head disappeared from view as she bent down. She rifled through her backpack. Slapping her notebook on the table, she straightened and said, "I think we've got a couple of cases coming our way."

Allison flipped through the pages.

I glanced at Hayden. "How are you doing?"

He slouched in his chair. "Fine."

"Are you sure?"

"Why wouldn't I be?"

"Your clothes are wrinkled," I said.

He shrugged. "I'm trying a new look."

"You're moody," said Allison, her head still bent over her book.

He glared at us. "There's nothing wrong with me."

Allison looked up. She pushed her glasses up her nose. "No one's saying anything's wrong with you. We're your friends—"

"Then be one and butt out of my business."

I held my hands up in surrender. "Fine. I was just asking." I looked at Allison. "Did you find your notes?"

She nodded then looked at each of us. "Things aren't so exciting with new cases coming in."

"I saw you talking to a whole bunch of kids," I said. "It looked like you were getting some business for us."

She wiggled her glasses. "You're not going to like it."

Hayden and I glanced at each other.

"We have a few choices. Madison said her concert T-shirt went missing from gym yesterday and she thinks Selena took it. Also, Peter says someone keeps stealing his chocolate-honey sandwiches from his lunch. Indra thinks Miller likes her and she wants us to find out. And the Lemon sisters are at it, again. This time, they both like Joe."

My face scrunched together. "Forget Indra and the lemons."

"I know you don't like those cases," said Allison. "But they pay. People always want to know if someone likes them—"

Hayden muttered something but I couldn't understand the words.

"What?" Allison looked at him. "I didn't hear what you said."

"Nothing," he muttered. "I didn't say anything."

"Okay," she resumed. "Anyway, I can work it on my own. It's pretty easy stuff—"

A hot-cold rush washed over me. Even though I still thought Sal was full of beans, every time Allison offered to work a case by herself, I felt weird. "I don't think we should split up."

"We're not splitting up, just using our strengths. You hate that love stuff, but well, I love it—"

Hayden muttered again.

"Seriously." She put down her pencil. "What is it?"

He shook his head. His eyebrows drew together and his mouth pulled into a sneer. "Everyone wants to know if someone likes them. But then what? What about after? What about—" He bit back his words. Hayden shoved his chair back and stood. "Forget it. Whatever you two decide is fine with me. I'm just a kid. I have to go along with what everyone says, don't

I?" He pivoted on his heel and stormed out.

"What the heck was that?" I stared after him.

"His parents." Allison's voice was quiet. "We probably shouldn't have hinted that we knew something was going on."

"I just asked him how he was doing."

"Yeah, but he obviously doesn't want to talk about it."

I stood. "Maybe I should find him and tell him I'm sorry."

She shook her head. "No, don't bring any more attention to it."

I flopped into my chair.

She sighed. "We have to give him space. That's what friends do. In the meantime, there are cases that need our attention."

I turned my focus from Hayden to work, but I couldn't get rid of the bad feeling in my stomach. It crawled up my chest and sat in my mouth like a rotten egg.

When I wasn't looking, Hayden had become a more than a friend, but one of my best friends. He was in a rough place and I didn't know how to help him. It made me feel like a failure.

****

Recess didn't go any better. Allison and I argued the whole time about whether to take the cases. Hayden just stood off to the side, his arms folded across his chest, a scowl on his face. I wanted to talk to him, but Allison kept my attention.

"We need the money," she said.

"Not that badly," I retorted.

"What's the big deal if I take the lead on them?"

"What's the—" Anger made me do a weird duck walk. "—because we're a team. We can't go around taking cases for ourselves. What's next? Two agencies?"

"Don't be stupid, Billy. Besides, we split up all the

time—"

"You're *both* being stupid!" yelled Hayden. "Fix it or I'm out of here!" He stormed off and headed toward the little kid's playground.

"Wow," said Allison, "I've never been told off by a six-year-old before."

I snorted. "I have a three-year-old sister. Try getting told off by a toddler."

She giggled, then turned to me.

Allison opened her mouth, but the bell—thank goodness—rang.

"We're not done, yet," she said.

I was afraid she'd say that.

****

Lunch came and I was no closer to a solution with Hayden. Plus, Allison and I were still fighting about the cases. I'd rather not have had work than take love mysteries, but she insisted on working for anyone who came our way.

I pulled on my jacket. Both problems would have to wait. Today was a half-day, which meant we got to go home at noon. I knew Allison would call and argue with me about expanding the agency. So, I ducked out of class and I didn't take my usual route. Allison would be waiting for me and I didn't want to fight—not until I got home and had a cup of hot chocolate. I thought about my partner and how much she'd push me to take those cases. I heaved a sigh. I'd need at least three hot chocolates to get me ready. Too bad my mom wouldn't agree. I'd be lucky to get two cups.

I pulled my gloves on and adjusted my toque. It had started snowing. Usually, I like playing in the white stuff, but with everything going on, I needed my strength. I couldn't let a cold or flu take me down. I zipped up my coat and hung a left.

And ran into Allison.

I skidded to a stop. My mouth hung open.

She rolled her eyes and grabbed my arm. Hauling

109

me down the hallway, she said, "As if I don't know you by now. We have to talk about the cases."

"Oh, man, and I didn't even get *one* hot chocolate."

"I have some money. I'll buy you some hot chocolate."

Tempting, but I knew she was only pulling out to the good stuff to bribe me. "No, thanks," I said in my best, tough guy voice. "I'll wait until I get home."

"Ugh. Come on, Billy. We need a case. The thing with—" She glanced around and dropped her voice. "Mrs. Smith worked out, but we can't tell anyone that. As far as the kids know, we haven't had a case in weeks. It's going to look bad if we don't get some work."

"But love cases? Can't we just hide someone's doll and get ourselves hired?"

She shot me a dirty look. "I told my mom I'm walking home with you. She's going to pick me up there."

I sighed. This was going to be a very long walk home.

We stepped outside. A blast of cold hit my face. The wind sprayed snow and the flakes hit my skin like sandpaper. I blinked hard to get the burning feeling out of my eyes. My vision cleared and I noticed all the kids staring in the same direction.

I followed their gaze and saw a familiar-looking gold Mercedes parked behind the three buses. It wasn't the luxury car that had everyone's focus. It was the man and woman, screaming at each other. He stood on the driver's side and pounded his fist on the roof of the car. She was planted on the other side and yelled back at him. Both of their faces were red, their eyes narrowed in fury.

The worst part wasn't screaming. It wasn't him yelling about how she didn't support him, or her yelling that he'd abandoned them. The worst part was Hayden, caught in the grip of the woman. He kept his head

110

down and his body turned away from the school.

"Mr. and Mrs. Small are at it, again," I said.

Allison snorted.

Mrs. Smith left her spot by the bus and walked briskly to where Hayden's parents were. Hayden tried to break his mom's hold and move to the car door, but she just yanked him back and yelled, "This is your son. You're embarrassing him. Are you happy, now?"

"Me?" Mr. Small's eyes went wide. "You're the one who's embarrassing him. All that garbage about him being a model. The kid's the size of a four-year-old—"

Allison hissed.

"—you think you're helping him?" Mr. Small jabbed his finger at his wife. "You're trying to live through him."

Mrs. Small snorted. "Well, you'd know all about that. What's the name of the—"

By this time, Mrs. Smith had reached them. She leaned in and said something to Mrs. Small. Hayden's mom turned and saw everyone staring at her. She wrenched open the back-passenger door and tossed Hayden inside. Then she got inside and slammed the door.

Mr. Small did the same. He revved the car and pulled into the road. The car raced down the street.

Allison plucked at my sleeve. "We should go."

Reluctantly, I followed.

****

We argued about the cases when we got to my house. Later that night, on the phone, we argued even *more* about the cases. Allison called it "debating the merits of the issue." I called it a giant headache. To make matters worse, my mom didn't let me have a third cup of hot chocolate. I nursed my half-empty mug and nibbled on a marshmallow.

"We should take these cases," said Allison.

"They're not my style."

111

"Martin Luther King Junior said that if a man is called to be a street sweeper, he should do such a good job that angels will praise his work."

Man, I hated it when she quoted people I admired. It was like she was using them against me. "Fine. Give me a street and I'll sweep it, but I'm not taking a love case."

She sighed. "Billy, it's not about the job. It's about the attitude. He's saying that even when you don't like the job, you do it to the best of your ability."

"I know what he meant," I ground out and took a swallow of my drink. The sugar shocked my system. Now that I was cutting back on junk food, it had a bigger effect on me. I coughed and sputtered.

"You okay?"

I grunted.

"We need to build the business and that means taking cases we'd rather not. But you have a choice, either you want to be a detective or you just want to play at being one."

"I don't *play* at being a detective."

"Everyone needs help, sometimes," she said, "even when we don't agree with their problem. These people want your help. Are you going to give it?"

I groaned. "People in love need mental help, not detective help."

"*Billy*—"

"Speaking of people needing help, what are we going to do about Hayden?"

"Nothing."

"What?" I sputtered. "But you just said—"

"He's not asking for help, Billy. If we push him, we could make him really mad. If we do that, how are we going to help him?"

I sighed. "I guess."

"Tomorrow," she said. "We'll see how he's doing. Maybe he'll be more open to talking to us."

"If you say so."

We argued for another ten minutes. Then my mom called for me to help with my sister.

"I have to go," I said. Then, in my best tough guy voice, I growled, "And we're done with this. No more love cases."

She snorted. "Nice try, Billy. We'll finish this tomorrow."

I gulped. She didn't even have to try at the tough guy voice. It just came naturally. I hung up and went downstairs to find my mom.

The next day, Hayden didn't show up at school.

When I pointed it out, Allison said, "Never mind. When my parents got divorced, I didn't go to school for a couple of days." She shrugged on her backpack, and pushed her chair under the table. "He'll get over it, but it will take time. His parents were pretty embarrassing. I'd miss a day of school, too."

"I guess."

Allison hadn't been at MacDonald as long as I had. She didn't know that Hayden had never missed a day of school. The kid loved learning. I couldn't believe he'd skip school because of his parents. Still, my folks weren't in the middle of getting a divorce. I trusted Allison knew stuff I didn't.

At lunch time, I learned how wrong I'd been. I was putting my books away and getting ready to line up for the cafeteria when the phone rang. Mrs. Robertson answered it, then looked at me.

Setting down the phone, she said, "Billy, Principal Lee needs to see you in her office."

I felt like someone had dumped an ice-cold bucket of water on me. No one wants to be summoned to the principal's office. I nodded and went to the door. The gaze of every kid in class followed me.

I made the long walk to the general office. When I arrived, the secretary told me to go right in. I did and found Allison sitting in one of the chairs by the table.

113

My breath left in a soft *whoosh.*

Principal Lee had six chairs in her office. Two were across her desk, four stood by the round table. If you were in trouble, you sat across from her desk. So, now I knew I wasn't in trouble. The question was: what was I doing here?

"Billy." Principal Lee stood and beckoned to the chair by her. "Come sit with me and Allison."

I glanced at my friend but she looked as confused as I felt.

After I sat down, Principal Lee said, "Have either of you heard from Hayden?"

I frowned and shook my head.

Allison said, "No, ma'am."

"What happened?" I asked.

Principal Lee hesitated.

My heart lurched. Adults take their time when they're not sure what to say. This was *not* good.

She smoothed her hands on her blue skirt and said, "When Hayden didn't arrive at school today, the secretary phoned to see if he was sick." She gave us a small smile. "You know, he's never missed a day."

"I know," I said quietly.

She took a breath. "His mom dropped him at school." She looked me in the eye. Then she looked at Allison. "Kids, Hayden's gone." She took another breath. "We think...we think he may have run away."

My skin went hot, then cold, then hot again. Running away? It was unthinkable. "Are you sure?" I croaked the words.

She nodded. "Is there anything you can tell me? Anything at all?"

"He was upset yesterday," Allison said, her voice quiet. "His parents were fighting in front of the school—"

Principal Lee's face tightened. "Yes, Mrs. Smith told me."

"I—Billy wanted to talk to him, but I told him it

114

was better to give Hayden some space." Allison's face crumpled. "When my parents got divorced, the last thing I wanted to do was talk. I thought...I thought I was being a good friend."

Principal Lee squeezed Allison's hand. "It's okay. You couldn't have known."

Allison swallowed but didn't say anything.

"The two of you have a special talent for finding lost things," said the principal. "I want you to ask around and see what you can find out." She held up her hand. "Be discreet. Do you know what that means?"

I nodded. "Don't let anyone know that he might have run away."

"That's right," she said. "Now, I know you normally get paid to find—"

I held up my hand. "No charge."

Allison nodded. "This is personal," she said, her voice thick.

"Okay," said Principal Lee. "Head back to class. At the end of the day, let me know what you've found out."

We left her office.

"I feel terrible," said Allison. "I—"

"Not now," I interrupted. "Later, you can feel bad. Right now, we need to find our friend."

We split up. I didn't bother eating any lunch. I don't think Allison did, either. We spent all our time asking kids if they'd seen him and checking the spots he liked to hang out. By the end of recess, we hadn't turned up any clues. By the end of the day, we hadn't found any sign of him. We reported our status to Principal Lee, then left school.

I wanted to go to the mall and Game-O-Rama and see if I could find him, but I'd promised my mom I'd come home right after school. I told Allison goodbye. Then I went home, feeling worse than the time I had the stomach flu. My friend was missing and I didn't know how or where to find him. What kind of detective did that make me? What kind of friend did that make me?

When I got home, I phoned my mom and told her what happened. She said she couldn't help me right away, but when she got back from work, we'd have dinner. Then, Dad and my brother would look after my sister. Mom said she'd drive me and Allison around. That made me feel better. I called Allison and told her. She said her mom had made the same offer.

And that gave me an idea.

I sent an email to every kid I knew. I told them that the detective agency was thinking of bringing in extra help, and there was a test for anyone who wanted to join. Then I told a lie. I said that Hayden was hiding and they had to find him. I also went on Buddy Link and posted the information. Within minutes, word had spread. Almost the entire school would be looking for Hayden.

I left my computer and stared out the window. The night was cold and dark, and Hayden was all alone. When Mom called me for dinner, I ate because I needed the energy, but I barely tasted the spaghetti and even the chocolate milk tasted like nothing. As soon as the dishes were put in the dishwasher, my mom tossed on her coat. The two of us headed to the car. I used my mom's cell to phone Allison as we drove. When we reached her house, she was already waiting on the porch steps with her mom.

Mrs. Ranger climbed into the front seat. "I wanted to help," she said. "Allison said it was okay to come along."

My mom nodded. "We need as many bodies as we can to look for him."

Allison sat behind her mom.

"Where to?" Mom asked as Allison fastened the seatbelt around her body.

"West Edmonton Mall," I said. "He really likes Game-O-Rama."

Mom drove. None of us talked. We were too

locked in our fears to say anything. Mom stopped at the entrance and said, "I'll wait here. The cell reception in the mall isn't good. I can call around to other parents and see if they found anything."

Mrs. Ranger unbuckled her seatbelt. "I'm coming inside."

"Mom, we can go alone," Allison said. "You don't have to come. We know one of the security guards. I think he'll let us use the cameras to look for Hayden."

Mrs. Ranger and my mom exchanged a look. It was hard to tell exactly what was going on. The car was dark and the lights from the mall weren't bright enough to light the interior of the vehicle. Still, I caught the vibe. There was something else going on. Something that neither Allison or I had thought about.

Mrs. Ranger hesitated. Her finger drummed on the dashboard.

My mom gave her a small nod.

Allison's mom turned around and said, "I don't know what's happened to Hayden. None of us do. Until we find him, I don't want you out in public alone."

The way she said it made the hairs on the back of my neck go up.

Allison grabbed my hand.

I didn't pull away.

"You think someone took him?" she asked.

"I don't know, sweetie," said her mom. "But he's only six and there are a lot of things that can happen when you're little. We have to be safe and be smart." The seatbelt slithered to its spot by the door. "Let's go." She stepped out and the cold, winter wind rushed in.

We followed her into the mall.

"Did you bring a picture of him?" asked Mrs. Ranger.

Allison nodded. So did I.

We asked every employee of the Game-O-Rama, showed them his picture, but no one had seen him.

Then we went to the security desk. Dennis was there and he let us use the cameras, but Hayden was nowhere to be found. Disappointed and even more afraid, I left.

"I was sure he'd have been here," said Allison.

"Me too."

"Let's ask the mall security," suggested Mrs. Ranger.

We spent an hour talking to the mall police, then another hour walking around. We even tried paging him, but nothing worked. If Hayden was hiding in the mall, then he was doing a great job of it.

"Let's go," I said.

Mrs. Ranger put her arm around my shoulder. "We'll find him."

"You don't know that," said Allison.

Her fragile smile broke. "No, I don't. But I have to hope." She looked at her daughter. "If anything—if you were miss—" Her voice cracked. She blinked quickly and turned away. "We have to keep trying. For Hayden and his family. We *have* to believe we'll find him."

Allison led the way to the exit. We rushed through the snowy night, our boots getting wet from the slush on the ground, and climbed into the warm, dry car.

My mom turned on the interior light and looked at us. "No luck, huh?"

I shook my head.

She gave me the kind of smile grownups give when they're terrified but trying to be brave. "Okay, let's try another place."

"Let me see where everyone else has looked." Allison pulled out her cell and logged into her Bulletin Board account from Buddy Link. She scrolled through the uploaded messages and posts from the kids who were searching for Hayden. "They've looked at every likely place." The skin on her forehead went into tiny wrinkles. "The movie theatre, the mall, the mini-put...where else can we go?"

"Maybe we've been going at this all wrong," I said

thoughtfully. "We're looking at the places a kid would go to have fun."

"And?" Allison closed her phone.

"Maybe we should look at places a kid goes to when he wants to be alone."

"The library?" suggested my mom.

"A coffee store?" asked Mrs. Ranger. "They have comfy couches..."

I shook my head. "People would wonder about a kid who's alone in a library or a coffee shop."

"Are you sure?" asked my mom.

Allison smiled. "You're not a kid, anymore, Mrs. Vale. But trust me, when you're a kid and you're in a grownup place, *everyone* notices."

"Where would he go?" Mrs. Ranger paused. "I suppose a fast-food restaurant. Lots of kids are there, but it's still a grownup place, isn't it?"

"Yeah," I said, my mind churning out one, unlikely but possible location. "But what if he was hiding at school?"

"At school?" Allison's eyes went wide. "Someone would have seen him."

"Not necessarily," I said. "Think about it. Until tonight, none of the kids knew he was missing. They could have walked right past him at school and not paid any attention."

"But the teachers—"

"You know how easy it is to hide from a teacher. There are the bathrooms, the nooks in the hallway, the spot under the stairs..."

Mom looked at the clock on the dashboard. "Maybe Mr. Franks, the caretaker, is still there. Let's go. If the school's empty, I'll try calling Principal Lee."

I nodded, my mouth suddenly too dry to talk. This wasn't just my only idea.

It was my last.

If Hayden wasn't there, I didn't know where else to

look. I glanced up at the night sky, at the thick, white flakes floating down from the black sky. It was cold, dark, and he was a kid who was all alone. I searched the sky. The clouds made it impossible to see any stars, but I still closed my eyes and made the most important wish of my life: that we would find Hayden and he would be okay.

****

Mom pulled the car into the first parking stall at the school. Then all of us got out and made our way to the front. As I turned the corner, I saw a dark figure moving toward the door. It was too large to be Hayden.

The person moved into a pool of light.

Mrs. Smith.

She turned at the sound of our footsteps.

"Jessie," said my mom. "What are you doing here?"

"Most likely, the same thing you are: looking for Hayden."

"What made you think of the school?" I asked.

"It's warm, there's food, and it's the safest place he knows." Her breath came out in thick puffs. "What made you think of it?"

"Sort of the same thing," I said. "It's quiet and he'd be safe."

"Let's hope we're both right," she said. She unlocked the metal doors and we stepped inside. "There are flashlights in the office." Her voice was quiet. "I don't want to turn on any lights. If I do, he'll know something's up."

We followed her shadowy figure to the storage room in the office. She gave each of us a flashlight.

"How should we look for him?" asked Mrs. Ranger.

"Vale and Ranger will be one team," said Mrs. Smith. "We adults will be another. We'll start in the cubicles—room sixteen—and work our way down. The kids will start on the other side of the school."

We nodded.

Mom and Mrs. Ranger went first. Allison and I followed, but Mrs. Smith grabbed my shoulder and yanked me back. Bending close to my face she said, "There are two places that he could be: the cafeteria and the library. Look there first."

I frowned, but not because of the coffee-garlic smell on her breath. "Why don't we go to one and you go to the other?"

The skin on her face softened. "Because he's six and he's mad at adults. He'll hide from us, but he may not hide from you."

"Oh." I blinked. "That's a good idea."

"Don't get used to it, Vale," she said gruffly. "We're working together on this, but only this. Come school time tomorrow, my eye will still be on you."

"I wouldn't have it any other way."

She grunted and went to catch up to the adults.

I raced to Allison.

"What did she want?"

"She thought we should check the cafeteria and library."

She eyed me. "Really? Smith's being helpful?"

"Kinda creepy, eh?"

"Tell me about it."

We walked in silence. The flashlight didn't do anything to light up the gloom.

"I feel like this is my fault," whispered Allison.

"What? Why?"

"You wanted to talk to him. I told you not to." Beside me, she shrugged. "Maybe it you'd talked to him, he wouldn't have run off."

I shook my head. "You can't blame yourself."

"Why not?"

"Because then I'll have to blame myself for not fighting harder *to* talk to him and I feel bad enough."

She swung the flashlight by her face and I saw her smile.

121

"Thanks."

"No problem."

We were almost at the library when she said, "I'm not trying to split up the agency."

I stopped. "What?"

"Earlier today, you said we shouldn't split the agency. I'm not trying to take over or anything."

"Oh." I shrugged. "Yeah, I know that."

"No...really." She took a breath. "The truth is, I don't really care about it."

I grabbed the flashlight and shone it in her face.

She squinted and pushed it away.

"You don't—"

"No, no," she said quickly. "I care. I just...don't care like you care."

"I'm confused."

She took the flashlight and shut it off. "So he won't see it and hide."

"Oh. Okay."

"I just meant—" She whispered. "I like the agency. I just—I just like hanging out with you, more. I would never split the agency because then I couldn't hang out with you and Hayden. That's why I do it." She stopped and took a breath. "Because you're my friends."

I thought about this. Then I thought about how wrong Sal had been. "Is that why you're pushing for us to take the love cases? Cause you think we won't hang out if we don't have a mystery to solve?"

"Yeah."

I could barely hear her. "Oh."

We stood there for a second.

"Tell Indra and those girls we'll take the cases."

There was a brief silence, then: "Okay." She moved to the library doors.

"Allison?"

"Yeah?"

"You don't need cases to hang out with me and Hayden. We're your friends and friends don't need an excuse." I couldn't see her in the dark, but I swear I felt her smile.

"Thanks, Billy." She went to open the door.

"Wait," I whispered. "Do you remember where the lights for the library are?"

"Yeah."

"Okay, let's go in quiet-like. Then you flip the lights. We'll never find him in the dark. If we shine the flashlight, he can just hide from us."

"Got it, Chief."

I grinned. I *knew* Sal had been wrong.

We crept inside and quietly shut the door. I heard Allison's hands moving along the wall. Then light exploded into the dark room. I blinked fast and caught a flash of color ducking under a table.

"Forget it, Hayden," I said. "We see you!"

Allison leaned into me. "Did we?"

I blinked fast. "I think so—I know I saw something." Moving past the entrance, I went toward the table. I bent down and saw Hayden, crouched under a chair.

"Aww—Hayden! Get out!" Relief mixed with anger. "Of all the stupid—"

"Billy." Allison put her hand on my shoulder.

I jerked away. "No. That was totally stupid, Hayden."

"I don't care! Just leave me alone!"

"I wish! We've been running around looking for you—"

Allison hip-checked me out of the way. Crouching down, she said, "He's been worried, Hayden. We all have."

"No you haven't," he said bitterly. "You've just been worried about yourselves. Arguing about the agency and not even caring about me—"

"That's not true." Her voice was firm. "We may have been fighting, but you're our friend. You're the one who didn't care."

His eyes widened. "WHAT!"

"You heard me. If you'd really cared about *our* feelings you would have known we were worried. And you would have talked to us. But every time we tried, you just got growly. That's not fair. That's telling us to leave you alone. You can't be mad at us just because we did what you thought."

He shook his head. "You're confusing me—"

"Hayden."

We jerked at Mrs. Smith's voice and Hayden bonked his head on the bottom of the table.

I looked behind me and saw her imposing figure at the entrance of the library.

"I'm sixty years old, young man, and I won't crouch. Come out from under there." Her voice boomed in the empty library.

Immediately, Hayden crawled out.

"Sit," she commanded.

All of us reached for a chair and sat, stick-straight.

So did she. "You ran away."

He didn't say anything.

"That was stupid thing to do," she said.

He flinched.

"But you're not a stupid kid," she continued, "and I'm surprised you'd do this." She sighed. "There are a lot of dangers—even hiding in the school. You're smart, but not so smart you can avoid being injured wandering along here, after hours."

He opened his mouth but she waved her hand.

"I know," she said. "I saw your parents arguing. I know how terrible it made you feel." She stared at him. "What they did, fighting like that in front of the whole school, you know what that was?"

He glanced at us, then said, "Stupid?"

"You're darn tootin' it was stupid. They're grown-ups. They should know better."

His body relaxed.

"You know what the problem is?"

He shook his head.

"They thought you were too young to get what was going on, right?"

He nodded.

"They didn't tell you they were thinking of a divorce because they thought you were too little to really understand—"

"It's not fair!" He burst out. "They treat me like I'm some stupid kid—"

"And you're not," said Mrs. Smith, "But as smart as you are, you're still a kid."

His mouth went straight.

For the first time, I saw a kind look on Mrs. Smith's face. It took out the wrinkles and brought light to her eyes.

"Hayden," she said, "Do you know what income tax is?"

He shook his head.

"What about mortgage, interest rates, or shovelling bylaws ?"

Again, he shook his head.

"So, do you agree that while you're smart, you may not know everything because you're still a kid?"

"I guess," he said grudgingly.

"Good. So, trust me when I say there's more going on between your parents than two grown-ups arguing about if you should model or not."

"What kind of stuff?"

She shrugged. "I don't know. They haven't told me. But, if you're okay with it, I'm going to talk to them. I think you should know a little more about what's going on. After all, this affects your life, too, right?"

He nodded.

"And I'm going to talk to them about getting someone—a grown-up—that you can see once in a while: a counsellor. You can tell them all the things you don't want to tell your parents or your friends."

He looked at us. "I didn't really give them a chance."

"They're here, now," said Mrs. Smith, her voice soft. "Why don't you try to talk to them. In the meantime—" She stood up. "I'm going to get their parents and yours. It's time you went home."

****

Twenty minutes later, Hayden was bundled into his parents' car. From the main entrance, I watched the red lights of the vehicle go into the distance.

Mrs. Smith came to stand beside me.

"That was really nice, what you did for him."

She grunted.

I took a breath, glanced at her, then looked away. "It really was."

"I learned my lesson from Trudy—Mrs. Larson." She clasped her hands behind her back. "I didn't tell her everything about the budget cuts and the problems with the school's furnace because I didn't want to worry her. That was wrong. If I'd told her what was going on, we could have been a team. Instead, I ended up making her my enemy."

"Is that why you're so mean to kids?"

She spun around and glared at me.

I took a step back but met her gaze. "You don't want us to worry about stuff, so you just boss us around instead of talking to us?"

She tried to stare me down but I wouldn't budge

"It makes it easier when you leave."

"Leave?"

"You're only here for nine years," she said, "then you go on to high school. Saying goodbye is hard. It's easier when I don't really know the kids."

"But it's not nicer."

She cleared her throat and looked away.

"Billy?"

I turned and saw my mom. She stood beside Mrs. Ranger, and Allison.

"We should go." She smiled at Mrs. Smith. "Thank you for your help, Jessie."

Mrs. Smith coughed and cleared her throat. "No problem. Go on and I'll lock up after you."

We went out into the cold.

I looked back at Mrs. Smith, standing all alone in the school. After we climbed into the car, I asked my mom, "Is it too late to go to the grocery store?"

She frowned. "No, but what could you want from there?"

"An apple, right?" asked Allison.

"You remembered, too," I said.

She nodded.

"Remembered what?" Mrs. Ranger twisted in her seat to make eye contact.

I didn't tell them about Mrs. Smith and her candy addiction. And I didn't tell them that underneath all her grouchiness, coffee-and-garlic-breath was a really nice lady. Instead, I said, "She told me once that kids used to bring her apples. And I told Allison."

"You want to get her an apple?" asked my mom.

"Yes."

My mom smiled at me from the reflection of the rear view mirror. "I think that's a lovely idea."

I took one final look at the school as Mom pulled away from the parking lot. Mrs. Smith stood in the open doorway. I lifted my hand. After a moment, she lifted hers.

Natasha Deen

The Not So Secret Case Files of Billy Vale, P.I

Thank you for purchasing
this publication.
For other wonderful stories,
please visit
www.natashadeen.com

Made in the USA
Lexington, KY
13 January 2019